PERFECT MATCH: THE DRAGON KING

PERFECT MATCH

I. T. LUCAS

MONA

*M*ona stood in line in her new six-inch heels and debated the wisdom of her latest impulse buy.

The shoes had looked phenomenal on the shelf, not to mention on her legs, and walking with them around the store, she'd convinced herself that they were reasonably comfortable considering the height, but now her feet were in agony.

These beauties were meant to perch on a shelf and evoke yearnings of a more glamorous life, but they were not meant for walking or standing in place while calculating how long it would take for a blister to form under her right big toe.

Whatever.

She could power through the pain.

There was more at stake than her vanity or silly fantasies of glamour. Appearances were a big deal in the advertising world, and if she wanted to get promoted one day, she needed to start by looking the part.

Besides, she might be just getting coffee, but at least she looked fantastic while doing so.

Surreptitiously shifting her weight onto her left foot and lifting her right foot off the floor, Mona hoped no one would notice her flamingo pose. As the pain subsided and she managed not to fall on the person standing behind her in line, she thanked the stars for the yoga class she had started six weeks ago.

It had been one of those 'holy crap, it's the New Year, and I need a resolution' decisions, but she was glad she'd chosen yoga. It was certainly better than the resolution her mother had pressured her to make. There was no way she was—

"What can I get for you?" the barista asked, her hot pink hair and nose ring distracting Mona momentarily.

"Oh, yes. I'm sorry. I didn't notice that it was my turn. Cool hair, by the way."

The young woman smiled. "Thank you. So, what's your pleasure?"

"Umm..."

The vast selection on the chalkboard hanging on the wall behind the barista presented too many options. Mona had been too busy thinking about shoes and New Year's resolutions to choose her drink before reaching the counter. The woman standing behind her huffed and shifted on her feet, probably not because she too was wearing sky-high heels but because she was impatient.

"Whatever you recommend," Mona blurted. "As long as it's sweet and caffeinated, that is."

Most baristas wouldn't have accepted the responsibility for choosing her drink. They would have thrown the question right back at her, but Mona had a feeling that the owner of the hot pink hair and nose ring was a daring, independent thinker.

"Do you like cinnamon?" the girl asked.

Evidently Mona had been right about her. "I love it."

"I've got just the thing in mind for you. You're going to love it." She picked up a paper cup and a black marker. "What's your name?"

"Mona Krasowitz."

The girl nodded and wrote Mona K. on the paper cup. "Is that okay?"

Krasowitz wasn't a mouthful, but knowing how to spell it was a different story.

"Perfect. Thank you."

"I'll call your name when it's ready." The barista set the cup aside and glanced over Mona's shoulder at the woman standing behind her in line.

Getting the hint, Mona scooted aside and scanned the coffee shop for a vacant seat. The place was packed, but she spotted a chair by the window and rushed to claim it before anyone else could beat her to it.

She sat down, and as she took the weight off her feet for the first time in three blocks and fifteen minutes, she almost moaned in relief.

The shoes hadn't been one of her best buying decisions, but she couldn't return them, so she would find a way to enjoy them somehow.

Note to self. Bring another pair of shoes to the office to replace the killer heels with something more manageable for coffee and lunch excursions that require walking.

As her purse buzzed, Mona pulled out her phone and groaned. She'd only been gone for fifteen minutes, and already a whole string of texts from work was flooding her screen.

Talk about bad choices and questionable compromises.

Why the hell was she sticking with a company that didn't respect her lunch break, her off hours, or her vacation time? They hadn't even given her and her team the freaking bonus they'd deserved after their last big ad campaign win.

It was the damn promotion the owner of the agency was dangling in front of her nose that kept her from looking for a different job. Once she got a private office and her own secretary, everything would change. Her secretary would handle all those damn texts and emails and call her only in case of real emergencies.

Talk about dreams.

"Sixteen-ounce whole milk, cinnamon dolce latte for Mona K.!"

"Coming!" She winced as she got back on her feet.

Holding the groan that was building momentum in her throat, she forced a smile as she collected her cup. "Thank you."

"You're welcome." The barista smiled back.

As she turned around to return to her chair, Mona stopped and gaped at the guy who'd stolen her seat.

What the hell, dude, seriously?

"Excuse me." She walked up to him. "I was sitting here."

"Jersey rules," he said without giving her the courtesy of even looking up at her.

Instead, he plunked a pair of headphones over his ears and pulled a computer out of his backpack. Ignoring her glare, he flipped it open and started typing.

Unless she wanted to make a scene, there was no way she was getting her spot back. It wasn't worth it. Confrontations were not her style, and if they weren't work-related, she preferred to avoid them.

Mona had enough drama dealing with all the divas in the advertising agency.

As she scanned the shop, she held little hope of finding another vacant chair. It was the lunch rush in

New York City, and everyone she looked at seemed under-caffeinated, hungry, and pointedly not about to make eye contact.

I'll just sit outside. It's a nice day.

It was a little chilly, but Mona had a nice coat to brave the cold.

Her Burberry had gobbled up most of her last bonus, but the long honey-colored trench coat was stylish and warm. Unlike the shoes, it was worth the splurge.

Stepping outside, Mona minced her way over to the nearest vacant bench and sat down. Her spirits immediately lifted as she took a long sip of the sweet, cinnamon-flavored drink.

Mmm, letting the barista choose the drink for her was definitely the right thing to do. If she ever got to helm an advertising campaign for a coffee company, she would use the hot-pink-haired barista with a nose ring as its ambassador and make this particular drink its flagship.

She would kill it.

The slogan popped into her mind next, ready to print in bold letters—*the sweetest luxury is the one we indulge in every day. Insert imagery of a beautiful woman lifting a cup of coffee to her smiling mouth.*

Delicious indulgence... No, that was too closely repetitive. What about... *delicious extravagance that can be yours if you...*

Bzzt. Bzzt.

Wait, what?

Bzzt.

Mona groaned. "Not again," she muttered as she pulled her phone out of her purse.

When a piece of crumpled paper fluttered to the ground, she reached down and picked it up. She was about to stick it in her pocket but decided not to. Perhaps she should put it in the trash instead of stuffing the pockets of her beautiful coat.

Unfolding the paper, she expected it to be an old receipt, but it wasn't anything as innocuous as that. What the beautiful cursive font spelled out was something Mona dreaded more than the walk back to the office in her six-inch heels.

Your Perfect Match Virtual Adventure awaits!
Redeem your token today at
www.PerfectMatchVirtualFantasy.com

MONA

*M*ona was tempted to put the note in the trash or at least shove it back into the depths of her purse where it could stay in perpetuity as far as she was concerned.

To bolster her resolution, she crumpled it and checked her phone, only to discover that fate was conspiring against her.

Gah. Mona took another sip of her latte to help hold her existential dread at bay as she opened her mother's text.

As usual, the text was two pages long.

Hi honey! There followed a paragraph about her mom's day, the wait she'd had at the bakery—ha, preach—and the way eggs were so darn expensive these days, and then she finally got to the point.

By the way, I called Perfect Match today to check whether you've redeemed your token, and they said it has yet to be claimed. Far be it from me to tell you what to do— okay, that was laughable—*but I feel like this is a wonderful opportunity for you to explore new horizons. Besides, it's only good for six months, and time is running out.* Yes, Mona knew that. Her mother reminded her of it every time they spoke. *It's not like signing up for an Experience would be an actual commitment to a real human being, you know.* God forbid. Rub it in, Mom. *But that token cost a lot of money, and I don't want your birthday present to go to waste. If you don't intend to use it, then consider giving it back to me. I wouldn't mind having an Experience with a charming older gentleman.*

"Oh, come on." Irritated to the point of acting atypically and calling her mother, Mona pressed the call button.

"Darling!" her mother trilled, sounding absolutely delighted. "How lovely to hear from you!"

"Mom," Mona interjected before her mother started an hour-long monologue about everything that had happened in her life since the last time they'd spoken.

"What's the matter? Oh, yes. I guess you read my text!"

How was it possible to cram so many exclamation points into every conversation?

After a lifetime of listening to Kaitlyn Krasowitz, Mona could see them punctuating the ends of all her mom's sentences.

"I did." She crossed her legs and hissed as she put

too much weight on the right foot. She re-crossed them on the opposite side. "Mom, I need you to give me a break about this Perfect Match thing. I don't have time to even read through their marketing materials."

The truth was that she was curious to see how they'd managed to get her frugal mother to shell out thirty-five hundred dollars for a token that could be redeemed for one virtual experience. Their advertising agency must have done an amazing job, and she might learn a thing or two from them.

But that was where her curiosity started and ended.

Mona wasn't interested in a glorified matchmaking service and what they had to offer. With how much they charged for their virtual experiences, their customers were probably entitled rich dudes, and she met enough of those at work. She didn't need to go out of her way to meet some more outside the walls of the advertising agency.

Her mother huffed. "I need you to stop dithering over something as simple as using the gift I got you to have some fun. Honestly, I don't know why you are so hesitant about this. You make lightning-fast decisions in every other part of your life. In fact, I sometimes worry about how little thought you give your decisions. Like that agency you are working for that doesn't appreciate the precious diamond you are. They are treating you like crap. Pardon my French."

"Mom!"

"Well, it's true. My point is that you are decisive in everything except dating. What are you scared of, honey? But I digress."

Evidently, her mother didn't know her as well as she thought she did. She should have seen her staring at the beverage selection earlier and not knowing what to pick.

"It's not easy out there, Mom. There are so many creeps and losers stalking the dating apps."

Her mother sighed. "Tell me something I don't know. But that's the beauty of Perfect Match. It's costly, so there are no losers, and since it's virtual, you don't need to worry about creeps. I know you're picky about men, but it's not even a date!"

Mona rolled her eyes. "I'm not picky. Is it a crime to be choosy when evaluating the person who might be your partner for the rest of your life?"

"Please." Her mother's voice went flat. "A date is not a commitment for life, Mona. Having a boyfriend doesn't mean you're going to marry the man. My God, if that were true, I'd have been married over ten times since your father died."

"Mom, I don't want to hear about your dating life!" A guy walking by heard that part and shot Mona a look of compassion. She gave him a nod and resisted the urge to just end the call and put a stop to her mother's tirade.

"At least I'm getting out there and meeting people! At my age, that's no mean feat, honey. And you're not getting any younger, you know. Thirty is a milestone birthday in a lot of ways, Mona. Your biological clock is ticking, and the longer you wait, the harder time you'll have getting pregnant. You should really have your first child before hitting thirty-five. God forbid you don't meet the man of your dreams until you're forty because the odds of unassisted pregnancy go way down at that point, and if you—"

"Mom, stop." Mona was beyond flustered and into discombobulated territory now. "Please don't talk about my hypothetical pregnancies. It's just, ugh. I can't do this with you every time we speak."

"I'll stop bringing them up when you stop ignoring the fact that you're just too picky when it comes to men." There were no exclamation points anymore. "You need to get your head out of the clouds and return to earth. There's no such thing as Prince Charming or Mr. Perfect, honey. No one will tick every box you've got in your mental spreadsheet. You need to focus on finding a nice guy with a good job who looks decent and doesn't have any congenital abnormalities because—"

As Mona rolled her eyes, she was thankful it wasn't a video call. "Mom, please."

"Because otherwise, you'll be forever disappointed, and I don't want that for you." They shared a moment of silence before her mother went on, "He doesn't have to look like that movie star you had a crush on for so long. What was his name?"

Hugh Jackman.

"The one who played Wolverine in all those movies you and your father liked so much…."

Hugh Jackman.

"Henry Johnson? No, that's not right. Harvey Jackson?"

"Hugh Jackman," Mona said woodenly.

The pain in her foot was nothing compared to the pain in her head at this point.

"That's the one! Don't waste time looking for a man who resembles that handsome actor. Heck, he probably doesn't look that good in real life anyway, and he's too old for you."

Mona closed her eyes. "He's a very nice man, and he's also a married actor. It's not like I dream of meeting him in real life." Which was totally a lie, but her mother didn't need to know that.

"Yes, well, of course you don't. I'm just saying that if you expect to meet someone who looks like that in real life, you'll be disappointed, but maybe you can create an avatar who looks like him in Perfect Match. Wouldn't that be the best of both worlds?" A sharp, ringing sound began to peal in the background. "Shoot, my quiche is burning! Talk to you later!" Her mother ended the call.

With a sigh, Mona returned the device to her purse.

Perhaps her mother was onto something.

Perfection didn't exist in real life, but it did in the virtual world, and a date with a Hugh Jackman looka-like sounded like fun.

3

BRUCE

One, two, three...

It was a smooth entrance to the bass line, and as Bruce set the tempo with his rhythm guitar and kept it going, the rest of his bandmates joined in. It was one of his newer compositions, and they had only played it a few times, so things still needed improvement.

He could hear the lag from Jacob. The guy was trying to figure out the fingering through the lead-in to the bridge, but that was fine. He would get there quickly, as he always did. Lead guitar chimed in with a twang, drums picked up the sound, and they were off to the races.

Set my feet and hold them fast, make it so this might just last...

The only thing missing was the vocals. Those had

always been Carrie's part, one of the few things she'd liked doing with his friends.

Can't let 'em know how much it hurts, can't let 'em know the fear...

It had been three months since Carrie had last sung with the band, three months since she'd suddenly decided that their relationship wasn't enough for her and she needed more, three months since she'd crushed his heart and stomped all over it.

Funny how it had been just great during the five years they had been together, but then out of the blue, it wasn't.

But had it really been great?

Perhaps he'd been too obtuse to notice the cracks that had started a long time ago.

Tie my feelings 'round my neck and say I love you, dear...

"Nothing ever changes with you," she'd scoffed on her way out. "You've had the same old house, the same boring friends, and the same dull job since we met. You even cut your hair the same way you did when you were twenty-four! The only thing that ever changes with you is how close you trim your beard and the brand of beer you keep in your fridge. I'm done waiting for you to catch up to me. I want to live!"

Catch up? Shit. He hadn't even known it was a race.

Bruce played the final part of the song on autopilot and was grateful when the last note sounded so he could get Carrie's voice out of his head.

"I like this one," Peter said, dark eyes pleased as he smiled at the rest of them.

Peter was one of those old boring friends Carrie had referred to. He and Bruce had been friends since high school and worked at the same tech company that they had gotten jobs in straight out of college.

"Me too," Jacob said a little ruefully. "But I need to practice my part more."

"No worries, man." Rashad clapped Jacob on the back. "You've got the hardest part. It's gonna take a little longer, but it's worth the work. It's a really good tune."

"It is," Danika said, "but it would sound great with the lyrics." She was the other software engineer in the group and, as of now, the only woman in the band. She must have realized why there weren't lyrics and blushed a split second later. "Sorry, Bruce. That was insensitive of me."

"It's fine." *It's not.* "I'm over her." *I still feel like I've been stabbed through the heart with a drumstick.*

Maybe if he told himself that it was getting better often enough, it would become true.

The truth was the acute pain that had twisted his insides when she'd left, making life intolerable for the first month or so, was gone. Nothing of Carrie's remained in the house, and they hadn't even talked over the phone since her dramatic departure.

If Bruce was honest with himself, which he tried to be, he missed having another presence in the house and her warm body in his bed at least as much as he missed her in person.

He also missed how the house had smelled when she'd been there, of expensive perfume, laundry softener, and the lotions she'd smeared all over herself.

Now it smelled stale, precisely how Carrie had described him and his life.

They had next to nothing in common. She was a voice actress and an influencer, and it had annoyed her to no end that he'd refused to get a designer dog or let her film their life and post it on social media.

Bruce didn't enjoy sharing his private life with the public. He was an engineer who geeked out over music and liked to chill in his off time.

The fact that he'd never once thought of proposing to Carrie could have been a sign that things between them hadn't been as great as he'd let himself believe. She'd been a fixture in his life, a roommate, someone to have easy sex with.

Come to think of it, that was probably the 'more' she'd talked about needing and why she'd left.

As a hand clapped his shoulder, Bruce jolted and looked up. "Hmm? What?"

"Do you know what you need?" Jacob asked.

"What?"

"A six-pack of beer and a night of video games."

Bruce grinned. "You've read my mind."

That was just what he needed to unwind and get his mind off Carrie.

The others seemed to agree, and as the five of them moved from the garage to the living room, Bruce went to the kitchen to get the beers while his friends settled in. When he returned to the living room with a six-pack in each hand, there was an empty spot for him in the middle of his slightly saggy couch.

He looked at Jacob, who was crouching next to the record collection. "Aren't you playing?" he asked.

"I'll sit this one out. My fingers are still sore from the last one." He chose an album and walked over to the record player.

Rashad joined him in the music corner, and the two of them got comfortable on the overstuffed beanbags.

As Bruce sat on the couch, Danika handed him a controller. "Prepare to lose, buddy," she said with a manic grin.

"Bring it on. What are we playing?"

"*Mario Kart 8*, baby!"

Damn, that wasn't his best game or his favorite. He shouldn't have gone for the beers and let Danika pick. She was a demon at Mario.

"Can't we just play *Call of Duty* again?" He clicked the screen on.

"Bruce, buddy, you need to branch out a little," Peter said from his other side. "If we let you, you would always pick *Call of Duty*. You can probably hear that theme song in your head when you go to sleep at night."

"I don't!" He often did, but that was none of their business.

"You totally do." Peter got an odd gleam in his eye. "You know what you need?"

"New friends?" he grumbled.

"No. You need a new adventure." Peter waggled his brows. "A Perfect Match sexy adventure."

Bruce rolled his eyes. "Not that again. It's invasive—"

"It's customizable."

"There might be needles involved—"

"There aren't any." Danika elbowed him in the ribs. "You're such a baby."

"None of you guys have tried it, so how do you know if all the hype is true?" Bruce huffed. "If I want a hookup, I can get it on Tinder without shelling out thirty-five hundred dollars on that shit."

"It's not just for hookups," Peter said. "I did it with Nancy for our anniversary, and it was the bomb."

"And you're only telling us about that now?" Danika punched Peter's shoulder. "What kind of a friend are you?"

"The best kind." He playfully punched her back. "I didn't want you to get jealous."

"Right." Danika grabbed a beer and popped the lid. "So, how was it?"

Peter smiled, probably because he was having

mushy thoughts about his fiancée. "Nancy loved it. We both did. We chose the Paris adventure and combined it with a mystery element. There was a murder at a fashion show, and we had to figure out the whodunit. Nancy loves detective stories and had a blast playing a part in the fantasy."

Everybody knew that Nancy was a diehard fan of mysteries. She told anyone willing to listen that her parents had named her after the book character Nancy Drew.

"Actually, with her birthday coming up...." Peter suddenly grinned. It was a look that made Bruce nervous. "Let's race, just you and me. Whoever wins, the other has to buy him a Perfect Match token."

Danika handed Peter her remote. "I'll take the next round."

It wasn't like her to be so generous. Something was up.

"Thank you." Peter switched places with her. "I need to win this one."

"Are you that hard up for cash?" Bruce deadpanned, but his heart began to race.

He loved challenges and winning, which is what made him such an exceptional software engineer and earned him a high six-figure income. There was no problem he refused to tackle, and he never gave up until he found a solution.

"You know I'm not, but I never say no to free money." Peter rubbed his hands. "Besides, if you win, then you'll have to do the adventure, and believe me, you'll thank me for talking you into taking the plunge."

"Or curse you," Bruce grumbled.

"I swear, you'll have a good time." Peter put a hand over his chest. "Would I ever lie to you?"

Bruce lifted a brow. "Sure you would. Remember when you told me I would look great with a mullet?"

"That doesn't count. It was in high school, and mullets were in."

"Okay, what about when you told me I could fix my car with an engine cleaner? The damn radiator blew up."

Peter scowled. "It's not my fault your car was such a piece of crap. I didn't know any more about cars than you did, so it was your fault for asking me for advice. And that was back in college. I can't believe that you are even bringing up those things from ancient history. And besides, that does not constitute lying."

The guy was a master at deflecting blame.

"Okay, so let's take an example from something more recent. You told me that I'd get over Carrie in no time."

As a long silence stretched over the room, Bruce regretted saying that last part. It wasn't Peter's fault that he was still moping over Carrie.

"Listen," Peter said with a gentle tone. "This idea isn't about you getting over her, all right? Grieving the breakup is going to take as long as it takes. All it's meant to do is give you something fun and completely new to try with no strings attached."

Translation: it won't be tainted by any association with Carrie, and I shouldn't think about starting a new relationship yet.

Well, duh. He wasn't ready.

"Fine," Bruce said. "But you better not throw this game just to make me win, so I will have no choice but to do this."

"Pfft." Peter made his 'who, me?' face. "When have you ever known me to throw anything? Balls, parties, games—I'm not a thrower."

That was true. Besides, Peter hated nothing more than losing bets, especially when he had to shell out money.

"Let's do it." Bruce logged on. He was about to pick out his standard Yoshi character when what his friends had said about him echoed in his head.

"Pink Gold Peach?" Danika laughed and toasted him with her beer. "Awesome choice, Bruce. Way not to let heteronormativity get in the way of your gaming."

"Does Yoshi have a gender?" Rashad asked as Peter chose Luigi.

Peter lifted a hand. "Y'all shut up. We're about to start."

Three...two...one...

Bruce could honestly say he'd never played such a

charged round of *Mario Kart* before. He was decent at the game, not great, but tonight he was better than decent. He was awesome.

Naturally, Peter beat him time and again anyway, and by the last round, it wasn't looking good for Pink Gold Peach.

"Yeah, here comes another trip to Paris with my—damn it!" Peter got too close to a Piranha Plant, which messed with him long enough for Bruce to secure victory.

He watched the celebrations on screen with a dry mouth.

Had he really just won against Peter?

"Well, congratulations," Peter said, seeming unbothered about losing thirty-five hundred dollars. "I guess you're going on a Perfect Match Experience after all."

"I guess so."

Bruce had a strong feeling that his friends had set him up, but since he couldn't prove it, he just lifted his hand for the round of high fives that followed.

Well, shit. I guess I'm going to have myself a virtual adventure.

4

MONA

"Maybe your mother is onto something," Grace said. "You should give it a go." She chuckled. "If someone gave me a token for a Perfect Match fantasy, I would go for it."

It was a rare day when Mona's thirty-something friends agreed with her sixty-something mother, but it seemed that the alcohol had loosened their tongues. Instead of commiserating about pushy moms, they'd switched to talking about her choosiness and how it affected her dating life or lack thereof.

"I know for a fact that you haven't been on any of the dating apps in over a month," Avery chided her. "You told me so yourself. Where are you supposed to meet guys? At work?"

"God, no. I'm never dating anyone from the advertising world. They are all such entitled divas." Mona took a disconsolate sip of her mojito. "I much prefer the anonymity of the apps, but the last guy I dated was such a dud that he soured me on the whole internet dating thing."

"What was wrong with him?" Janet asked.

"He lived with his mother and grandmother."

"That's not so bad," Janet murmured, hiding her flaming cheeks behind her mimosa.

She was still living at home with her parents, albeit in the converted garage in the back, but still. The woman was thirty-two years old, and she made decent money. She could afford rent in the city and avoid her parents scrutinizing every guy she invited to her so-called cabana.

"And the one before that?" Grace asked. "What was wrong with him?"

"He chewed tobacco. Gross."

Grace rolled her eyes. "And the guy before that?"

"He..." What had his issue been, again? "He was vegetarian. I like bacon too much to date him. When he dropped me off at my place after we had dinner, I ordered a double burger delivery from Grubhub. I was so damn hungry."

Laughing, Emma shook her head. "You are too picky, girl."

"Too choosy," Janet said. "So what if you can't eat bacon in front of the guy? That's such a small sacrifice to make."

"Maybe." Mona leaned back. "If Bill had been great in every other way, I might have given up bacon for him. But frankly, he wasn't worth it. I hated his sancti-monious attitude, and his nasal voice grated on my nerves." She shivered. "I couldn't wait for the date to be over, and when he walked me to my door, I pretended to have a coughing fit so I wouldn't have to kiss him."

"You're so demanding and fussy," Grace said. "No one is perfect."

Mona waved a dismissive hand. "It's either right or wrong. There are some things I'm not willing to compromise on, and I refuse to feel guilty about it."

"Oh yeah?" Janet arched a brow. "It seems that you are adamant about your guy checking all of your boxes, or it's a no-go."

"Not true." Mona grabbed a tortilla chip and stuffed it in her mouth. "There are things I don't care much about."

Her friends' comments had made her uncomfort-able, and she always turned to food when she felt out of sorts.

"Like what?" Janet pushed. "What are you willing to compromise on?"

"I don't care about money. He doesn't have to be rich, but he does have to have a job. I'm not dating out-of-work losers who expect to mooch off me." She lifted a finger to shush her girlfriends. "And don't you dare tell me that's too much to ask for."

"It's not." Grace sighed. "But these days, so many people are being laid off that you can't hold it against a guy. The economy is shrinking, and even computer engineers are getting downsized."

"There is always work for those who are able-bodied and willing. I don't care if the dude cleans floors while waiting for a good position to become available, as long as he's not sitting at home and mooching off his parents or girlfriend."

"Fine. Let's put that one aside." Grace put her glass down. "What else are you willing to compromise on?"

When Mona's list of possible compromises was painfully short, Emma crossed her arms over her chest. "Where is the only place you can find exactly what you are looking for?"

"Where?" Janet asked with hope shining in her eyes.

"Perfect Match Virtual Studios," Emma smirked. "A custom-tailored dude is the only man who will meet Mona's requirements."

Janet sank back in her seat. "I was hoping you'd found a great new dating app."

"I did. Perfect Match is the best out there, but it's too damn costly." Emma smiled at Mona. "You have a token. Just use it."

Mona fingered the voucher in her purse.

Maybe her mother and her friends were right, and Perfect Match was precisely what she needed to restart her dating life.

5

MONA

*M*ona hadn't been thinking about Perfect Match when she'd gotten home later that night, she hadn't had time to consider it the next morning on her way to work, and then she'd been too busy with client meetings, art requests, and portfolio updates.

In fact, she'd completely forgotten about it.

She also hadn't thought about it when she'd gotten home and made her favorite comfort food, a chef salad with extra bacon. It hadn't even crossed her mind as she clicked the television on and watched two episodes back-to-back of her favorite romcom show.

Neither did it live in her brain rent-free while she drew a bath with Epsom Salt for her feet and chilled with a glass of wine for half an hour.

Liar.

Darn it, she was going to do it, and her mother was going to give her smug looks for the rest of her life.

Maybe she should come up with such a far-fetched fantasy that no one would want to share it with her, or if anyone did, it wouldn't be a fun experience. It was almost worth it just to avoid hearing endless *I-told-you-sos,* accompanied by *mother-knows-best,* and sprinkled with *you should always listen to your mother—she has your best interest at heart.*

Mona sighed, got out of the bath, wrapped herself up in her old fluffy terrycloth robe, and padded to her desk.

For a long moment, she stared at her laptop, debating whether she should open it or leave it closed and go to bed, but the truth was that she'd already decided and just hadn't womaned up to it.

"Yeah, Mona. Grow a pair."

She flipped the laptop open and typed in the Perfect Match URL. She didn't even need to look at the card. Who could forget *www.PerfectMatchVirtualFantasy.com?*

After going through all the tedious stuff like her name, date of birth, how she heard of them, blah, blah, blah, she signed the disclaimer and finally got to the good stuff.

Are you ready to choose the Experience of a lifetime?

"Your copy people are good," Mona muttered as she began to look through the offered Experiences.

She veered away from the real-world settings

because those didn't interest her. If she had found what she wanted there, she would have done it already and wouldn't be booking a virtual reality adventure.

The fantasy and science fiction settings were what she was going for, but the setups all seemed a little off to her. It wasn't that there was anything wrong with them, but it just felt odd to live through someone else's story instead of her own.

Scanning the page, she found what she was looking for at the very bottom.

"Custom Experience. Heck yeah!" Excitement bubbled up in her chest.

There had been a time in Mona's life when she'd been determined to become a great writer. She was going to create worlds people could get lost in—places they would love to visit repeatedly. She would be a beloved author and have thousands of readers waiting with bated breath for her next book. Getting a huge contract and being a *New York Times* bestseller also featured heavily in this dream.

It hadn't worked out.

Turned out that school loans got paid off a lot faster when working in the corporate world, and the job took so much of her creative energy that Mona hadn't had the chance to do any writing for fun in months.

Or was it years?

It was a depressing thought, but for once, the fire

in her chest was enough to push it away. If there was ever a time to dust off her writing muscles, this was it.

When would she get the chance to live a story of her own making again? And with her perfect guy?

Well, he wouldn't really be perfect, of course. Whoever they ended up partnering with her would have to fit the role she wrote for him, but he wouldn't really be like that.

After all, this wasn't real. It was fiction, and that was fine.

First, though, Mona had to figure out what kind of adventure she wanted.

Hmm.

Her fingers hovering over the keyboard, she let the question percolate in her mind for a few minutes. Maybe it would be easier to figure out what she didn't want from her Experience and go from there.

What hadn't she liked about the scenarios on offer? Probably the fact that they all seemed to play into the trope of the kick-ass chick who dreamed of riding into battle or ruling a country or saving a prince from a dragon, or all three at the same time.

Even for a fantasy, it was too unrealistic. Suspension of disbelief could only get her so far.

Besides, Mona wasn't some kick-ass Wonder Woman, nor did she want to be. She'd rather have super brains than super muscles and to outsmart the dragon rather than slay him.

After all, blood and gore didn't go well with a romantic adventure.

Well, maybe for someone else, but definitely not for her.

Heck, she wouldn't even ride the train, much less saddle up on a prancing steed.

But saving a prince...hmm.

What if the prince was the dragon?

What if he had been cursed, only instead of a curse, he looked at it more like a blessing? Maybe not at first, but with the help of a certain heroine's brilliant perspective...

Yes, yes! This could work.

Oh yeah, this was going to be good.

No, it was going to be great!

Epic!

If ever there had been a time in Mona's life for an epic moment, this was it! She was going to write her own beginning, middle, and ending.

And damn if it wouldn't be a happy one, too.

As the cursor blinked at her alluringly, Mona grinned, settled in her ergonomic chair, and began to write.

Once upon a time, there was a prince whose country was under siege...

6

BRUCE

*A*fter Bruce saw his friends off that night, he'd tried to pick up with his regular routine of stowing the music gear, cleaning up the beer cans, starting the dishwasher, showering, and then bed.

The simple tasks were so familiar that he could have done them with his eyes closed, but he'd been so distracted by his unexpected win that his guitar had ended up wrong side down in its case, the empty beer cans had landed in the dishwasher, and he'd turned the water in the shower to cold instead of warm.

Thankfully, the next day at work had flown by without him thinking about Perfect Match or whether he should even accept the token from Peter.

There was no doubt in Bruce's mind that his friends had conspired for him to emerge victorious to push him into going for it, but he could refuse to play along. Except, now that he was back home, he couldn't stop thinking about it, and even his guitar couldn't command his full attention.

Exasperated, he put it on its stand instead of attempting the case again and went to his home office.

Firing up his desktop, he found the Perfect Match website. "Let's see what the fuss is all about."

A few minutes into his perusing, Bruce was duly impressed. If what they claimed was real, the technology behind it was mind-boggling. It was years ahead of anything he was familiar with.

Maybe he should snoop around and see if they needed more programmers.

His job was great, but he would quit it in a heartbeat and even take a pay cut to have access to the Perfect Match technology.

"Slow down, Bruce," he chided himself.

First, he needed to go through the Experience to see if it was all the website promised, and if it was, he could then check whether they were hiring.

From what he'd seen so far, though, the adventure should be incredible.

He could do almost anything and be almost anyone he wanted to be. Best of all, he didn't have to do it alone or come up with the entire story himself.

Someone else would be living through the fantasy with him—a real woman who found whatever it was he chose interesting enough to give it a try, unlike Carrie, who'd taken the one thing Bruce loved more than anything else and made it all about her.

Not the Rock Star Experience, then.

Screw that.

It was too closely associated with his ex.

He needed something completely different, something Carrie would have never even imagined, and he needed to do it with someone who was her exact opposite.

No Carrie Version 2.0 for him.

There was a long list of adventures to choose from, from the mundane to the extraordinary and all the way to the bizarre, but nothing caught Bruce's fancy until he reached the very end and found a fantasy that made him laugh out loud.

"Werewolf adventure!" He chuckled. "Howl at the full moon, slink through the shadows, and revel in the power of the wolf inside the everyday hero."

He could have real fun with that, especially in light of the grief Carrie had given him over being too hairy and refusing to do anything about it.

"What are you, a werewolf?" she'd actually said once. "You're not even thirty, and look at you!" She'd waved a hand at his hairy chest and made a face as if it was the grossest thing she'd ever seen. "You have to do something about this fur!"

She'd even made an appointment for him at a laser hair removal place.

Reluctantly, he'd gone to the salon, but the technician had taken one look at him and shook her head.

"You're too young for this to be effective," she told him with a frown. "With the amount of testosterone that you produce at your age, it will grow back. Besides, your hair is too pale for a laser treatment. You should consider electrolysis if you want to proceed despite my advice."

No, thank you.

Getting his follicles invaded by a tiny needle and zapped with electricity until they died wasn't his idea of fun.

Carrie just couldn't appreciate a hirsute gentleman, but there was someone else out there who not only didn't mind hairy dudes but was actually fantasizing about meeting one.

Bruce created a profile, then checked "yes" on the werewolf adventure.

What followed was a questionnaire so intrusive that he doubted the FBI or CIA required that much information from new recruits applying for agent positions.

The conspiracy theorist in him imagined foreign interests searching for people who matched a certain profile or maybe even aliens searching for their long-lost descendants.

Bruce had been told that he had a wild imagination for a software engineer, but it still wasn't good enough to develop a story for his adventure. He would have to fill up the damn questionnaire and let the AI design one for him.

Are you willing to consider other shifted forms? the questionnaire asked.

Um…sure?

As long as it wasn't a slug creature who moved at the speed of molasses flowing uphill, then yeah. He checked that box, and the thirty-six that followed before moving on to the next section.

Describe the ideal partner for your chosen Experience.

That was easy. Anyone who looked nothing like Carrie.

Damn, he should do better than that.

With a sigh, Bruce threw a hand over his eyes, forcing himself to stop and think.

It was easy to let emotions get the better of him when it came to his ex. Right now, he needed to visualize his perfect partner, but he'd been with Carrie for so long that he couldn't imagine anyone else.

Perhaps starting with what he didn't like about her would lead him toward what he wanted from his ideal partner.

He didn't like Carrie's negativity. He didn't like that for the past year the only conversations they'd had were about what she wanted him to be doing differently. He didn't like that she blamed him for everything that wasn't going right in her life, and he didn't like the disappointed expression on her face whenever she looked at him.

He didn't like how he'd felt when he was around her, being constantly reminded of all the ways in which he was failing her.

She had made him feel small.

And it didn't help that logically, he knew it wasn't true.

His friends loved him, his bosses and co-workers appreciated him, and he was a damn good musician as well.

Bruce began typing.

My ideal partner will be happy with herself and able to accept others without wanting to change them to fit her unrealistic expectations. She'll be funny, adaptable, and willing to listen. She will communicate her needs clearly and not expect others to guess what she wants and then accuse them of not caring enough about her. She'll be smart, confident, and fun.

As for what she looked like...anything but a blonde.

He checked the next fifty-two boxes that had to do with appearance as optional because he really didn't care what size bra she wore or how tall she was, or what color her eyes were. He was okay with whatever avatar his partner chose. It surely wasn't going to be hideous, and he actually wanted to be surprised.

The following section was all about him.

Describe your ideal avatar for your chosen Experience. Who do you want to be?

Oh, damn. The following questions were even worse than the preceding ones.

Was a deep, intensive psychoanalysis part of the process?

Some of the questions forced Bruce to think about things he hadn't imagined contemplating when he'd gotten out of bed that morning.

It's just a fun, interactive experience.

It was no different than creating an avatar for a video game, right?

It didn't have to be any more profound than that.

Huh…so who did he want to be?

When Bruce closed his eyes and concentrated, the first image to spring into his mind was a character from a video game he'd envisioned creating back in college before established companies with deep pockets had lured him away into the corporate world.

The protagonist was a warrior, a leader. Someone with a commanding presence and the kind of charisma that made people follow. A physically attractive guy, someone that men emulated and women swooned over. A person who was strong enough to take care of the people who needed him without falling prey to their fears and manipulations. Someone who would do the right thing no matter what.

Perhaps he'd been subconsciously inspired by Wolverine because he envisioned his protagonist as a werewolf or some other shape-shifter.

The transformation aspect just felt right to him.

He wasn't great at verbalizing the visual images his mind created, so coming up with the right words to describe his avatar was difficult.

By the time Bruce was done with that portion, he was exhausted and decided to leave the rest of the questionnaire for the next day.

Hitting save, he let out a breath and leaned back in his chair.

It was better to take his time than make mistakes he would later regret. This could be the adventure of a lifetime, and he wanted to make it spectacular.

7

MONA

*M*ona had forgotten just how rusty her writing muscles were. By the time she managed to produce a satisfactory draft, the clock on her laptop blinked five-fifteen in the morning.

After consuming an entire pot of coffee over the course of the night while cursing under her breath as she'd written and rewritten things on her notepad, all Mona had to show for it was a measly thousand words.

It was a reminder of the other reason she'd chosen a career in advertising as opposed to life as a novelist. At the rate she was writing, she would never make enough money to survive on.

Ugh, why hadn't she remembered that before starting on this writing project?

Oh, right. She wanted to live out her perfect

fantasy with her perfect partner and didn't want anyone else to write her story for her.

Reading over what she'd written, her face contorted with the manic glee of a woman who was going to be regretting her life choices in a few hours, but for now was riding a wave of endorphins taller than the Statue of Liberty.

It was the witching hour, or so they said.

The prince hoped so because he desperately needed the witch, and finding her cottage was challenging. The sack slung over his shoulder contained gems and jewels from his family's treasure vaults, some of them dating back to when the kingdom was founded, but if she granted his wish in exchange, he would gladly part with his family's heirlooms.

Laying his offering on the ground, he called out, "Rozia, Rozia, Mistress Rozia! Please come out. I need your help."

The trees rustled, and the prince heard a great "stomp, stomp, stomp" approaching him.

Was the witch a giant?

Was he about to be squashed for his impertinence?

But no, the cottage was advancing toward him on four long stilts. Looking closer, the prince saw that the stilts were actually made of bone, and he shivered thinking of who they'd belonged to, but he stood his ground and waited for the cottage to settle down.

The structure seemed to exhale, and a moment later, the door opened, and a woman came out.

She was so unearthly beautiful that looking at her made his heart ache with longing. That was when the prince knew more than ever that he should be careful, or else he would fall under one of the witch's enchantments before he could hope to save his kingdom.

"Sweet prince," she said as she stopped before him, a smile on her heart-shaped face. "Tell me what troubles you, my darling."

Ignoring her coquettish demeanor, he told her about his kingdom. "My father is ill, and Trieste is in danger. Emboldened by the king's lingering illness, the vultures are gathering at the borders, ready to bite our kingdom apart. There are too many fronts to fight off at once, and it sickens me to watch my people die needlessly."

She smiled sadly and put her delicate hand on his arm. "That is indeed a dire situation, my prince. What do you wish of me?"

"I wish to become a dragon," he said. "No one would dare attack Trieste with a guardian like that on her borders. As a dragon, I could fly from one battlefield to the next in time to make a difference."

"That will take potent magic." The witch glanced at his offerings with her lips twisting in disdain. "Do you truly think that these trinkets are enough to cozen me into helping you? You will have to do better."

"I will give up everything to save my people," the prince said desperately. "What would you demand of me?"

The witch's smile chilled him to the bone, but the words that followed would freeze the blood in his veins.

"Your firstborn child, of course," she said.

The prince had known the witch's price would be steep, but he hadn't imagined a demand this heartless.

Still, did he have a choice?

Too many children were already dying, and the life of a potential future child could not outweigh them. Besides, it was in his power to refuse to marry and produce an heir. He could appoint one of his distant relatives as his successor.

"So be it," he said. "To save my people, I need the power of a dragon, and if you give me that, I will give you my firstborn child in exchange."

"Excellent," she purred as she caressed his arm. "Your sacrifice will be the stuff of legends, and your people will sing about their courageous prince for centuries to come. Dragon and fierce protector by day, a human by night."

The prince frowned. "What if my enemies attack at night?"

"Then you will have to rely on your soldiers," Rozia said flippantly. "If you stay as a dragon a full day and night, you will lose your humanity forever." Smiling, she pulled him toward her with surprising strength for such a delicate-looking maiden. "Let us seal the bargain with a kiss."

The prince let the witch do as she wished, and as she leaned in and kissed him, her lips were just as cold as her black heart.

He shuddered...then kept shuddering as a strange, fiery power flowed into his body. He wrenched away from her just in time for his bones to break apart and remake him into a...

"Return to me when Trieste is saved," Rozia called out as she watched him spread his new wings. "Don't make me hunt you down, my darling prince. It would make me very angry, and you don't want to see me when I'm angry."

Her words echoed in his head as he flew to the closest battlefield, but they faded as he laid waste to his enemies.

At first, his troops panicked and scattered, just like their foes, but when realization set in that the fierce dragon was fighting on their side, they rejoiced, regrouped, and regained all ground lost, pushing the invaders back beyond the border.

He became known far and wide as the Black-Winged Prince, and soon those eager to make war were just as eager to sue for peace. After only a month, he returned to the witch's clearing where her cottage still sat where she'd brought it with her magic.

"Now," he said as Rozia approached him, "I'm ready to be done with this transformation. Take your powers away so that I might be solely human again."

"Ah, my darling prince. That wasn't part of the bargain." Rozia caressed his arm with her cold fingers. "You asked to be a dragon warrior, and I granted your wish. If you want me to take my magic back, you must marry me and make me your queen."

The prince reeled back, stunned. "What? That wasn't part of the bargain we made. I won't do that. I can't!"

"Of course, you can! Why else would I ask for your firstborn, hmm? Do you think I eat babies for breakfast?" She laughed maniacally like the witch she was. "Your firstborn will be mine because I will be her mother, and one day she will rule Trieste." Rozia ran a long, sharp fingernail down his chest. "I assure you that once you make me your queen, our kingdom will never be threatened again."

Visions of dark magic flooded the prince's thoughts, and he knew he could never give in to the witch, no matter how alluring her promises sounded.

"No. I refuse." He forced her back, then pulled his sword. "Touch me again," he snarled, "and I will water the ground with your blood. I would rather be a dragon by day for the rest of my life than make you my wife and the mother of my child."

"How dare you speak to me thus?" Rozia raged. "I gave you everything you asked for! You ungrateful brute. You made me a promise, and you and your country owe me this and much more!"

"I promised you my firstborn," the prince corrected. "But I do not intend to ever sire one."

The witch narrowed her eyes, then spat between them on the ground, the gobbet of saliva hissing and blackening the grass. "Time will change your mind, princeling. As everyone you love will age and die, you will remain as young as you are now, and the only constant in your miserable life will be me." She smiled. "In your loneliness, you will return to me and beg to be mine. Once you tire of this life, find me and make me your wife and queen, and I might consider removing the curse when our bargain is fulfilled, and my belly swells with your child."

Then she and the cottage vanished.

Oh, heck yeah, that was epic.

8

MONA

"*H*i, I'm Leann." The Perfect Match technician led Mona to what looked like a dentist's chair. "Are you excited?"

"Of course. Isn't it obvious?" Mona asked. "I've been waiting for almost two weeks to get a match, and with every passing day, I've gotten a little more anxious. My fantasy experience is unique, and I was afraid no guy would want to share it with me." She smiled sheepishly. "When I finally got the notification that the Experience was a go, I booked the first available spot."

Her feelings about using her mother's voucher had done a complete 180 after she wrote out what she wanted to be a part of. She'd expanded the original version a bit, answered a few technical questions from the people who crafted the Experiences, then settled in to wait for a match.

For a while, Mona had worried that she was asking

for too much. After all, what kind of person wanted to be transformed into a dragon?

Was that even a thing?

Even if they were a dragon for only half of the time, that could be kind of a, well...drag, not to put too fine a point on it. Then again, maybe being a powerful, fierce, magnificently protective dragon prince was right up someone's alley.

Turned out she'd been right, and getting matched had felt like the ultimate validation to her.

"It's totally not a problem, as long as you don't bounce right out of the chair," Leann replied. "What sort of an adventure are you looking forward to today? It must be a good one—honestly, many people wait *waaay* longer to make a match."

"It's one I designed myself," Mona said, feeling pretty proud of herself. "It's a fantasy setting, and there's a kingdom and a dragon who's also a prince, and I'm not entirely sure who I'm going to come in as, but it's definitely not going to be as the wicked witch." Which made her wonder... "Do people ever come in and, like, set themselves up to be tyrants lording their power over the populace?" Because she had a boss who would probably like to play that role, honestly, but the idea of being stuck with someone like that in an Experience made her wince.

Leann shook her head. "I'm not one of the official Experience coordinators, so I can't say for sure, but I can tell you that the screening process for this is pretty darn rigorous. I don't doubt that plenty of folks have asked, but this is meant to be fun for both of the people involved. Perfect Match wasn't made to provide an outlet for people's worst impulses. The guys who founded the company are very upfront about the integrity of what happens here."

"So, I don't have to worry that my dragon prince is going to morph into a villain and put me in a cage or throw me into a volcano or something," Mona said, laughing nervously. It wasn't something she'd thought to be nervous about until the prospect was staring her in the face, but now...now she was glad to be getting some reassurance.

"Not at all," Leann said. "There are safeguards in place to ensure that neither you nor your partner experiences any debilitating mental or physical distress. Yeah, there might be some uncomfortable moments in there, but it's nothing that will scar you for life, I promise. We wouldn't have so many repeat customers if that was the case." She paused for a second, then added, "You know, your fantasy might not go exactly the way you've imagined it. We have to consider and incorporate what your match asks for as well."

"Oh, I know." If there was one thing Mona was good at, it was watching something she'd envisioned and put together from the ground up get changed into something else—that was the way of the world in her chosen career. No idea was sacred, and she was okay with that. "That's fine. I know it's more of a jumping-off point than a blueprint."

"Well, you sound like you're all ready to go, then!" Leann checked the IV line, then glanced at her computer. "Let's go through the safety precautions."

"Yes." Mona let out a breath. "My safe word is peaches."

Leann grimaced. "That's not good. What if you want to eat peaches while in the Experience?"

"I hate peaches. That's why I chose the word."

"Ah, then it's okay. What's your avatar's name?"

"Charlotte," she said.

"Any last name?"

"Do I need one?"

"Not really." Leann typed on her keyboard. "I see that you didn't choose family members or friends, but the system might provide them for you. Is that okay?"

"Of course." It would be interesting to see who the artificial intelligence would create for her.

"Excellent. We're all ready to go, so just relax, close your eyes...and remember to have fun there."

Mona grinned. "I will."

This was going to be the most fun she'd ever had. She couldn't wait to meet her prince.

9

BRUCE

*B*ruce was surprised at how easy and chill everything was.

The questionnaire had been super thorough, the physical had been a necessity given that he was going into an all-consuming, as-real-as-life virtual adventure, and the drive to downtown Manhattan had been predictably sucky. But actually, being inside the building, talking with the people setting things up... was cool.

The Experience coordinator, a leggy blonde who reminded him too much of Carrie, just without the attitude, led him inside a room that looked like a futuristic dentist's office.

"This is Brian," she introduced the technician. "He's going to take care of you today."

Bruce offered the guy his hand. "Nice to meet you."

"Same here." Brian shook his hand as his eyes roved

over his sweatpants and T-shirt. "I see that you followed instructions and dressed comfortably. You can remove your shoes and put them in the cubby over there." He pointed at a corner of the room set up with a hook and hanger, a cubby for shoes, and a comfortable-looking armchair to sit in while taking off or putting on the shoes.

Luckily, Bruce had worn a new pair of socks with no holes in them, so he could take the shoes off and get comfortable.

"You're going to love it." Brian reclined him back. "I've been with Perfect Match ever since the days they were still beta testing it." He made quick work of hooking Bruce up to the IV. "It hadn't been a smooth ride, and the founders had nearly given up on the idea after sinking all their money into it."

It was such a typical story. Out of every ten startups, less than a handful made it.

"How did they save it? Did they have a breakthrough?"

The tech shook his head. "They sold part of the company to a silent partner to get an infusion of funds, and the partner brought a genius programmer on board who solved all of the technical kinks. Without him, we wouldn't be here today."

"Fascinating. What's the programmer's name?"

Bruce knew most of the big names in the industry, but if the genius was from another country, he might not have heard of him.

Brian shrugged. "He only introduced himself as William, and even though he talked up a storm, he never mentioned his last name. Nice guy, though."

"I don't know any famous programmers who are named William, or Will, or Bill." Bruce frowned. "Was he a foreigner?"

"I think so. He had a Scottish accent. Anyway, what I wanted to say is that I've tested most of the standard environments, and they were all incredible. You have nothing to worry about."

"Glad to hear that, but I'm not worried. I've heard good things about the Paris adventure. Did you get to try it?"

Bruce felt a little bad about spending Peter's money on what was essentially a mental vacation for himself, but then again, it hadn't been his idea. Peter had insisted.

"I did." The tech frowned. "Wait, you're not doing that one, are you?" He picked up his tablet and began to scroll quickly. "I have you down for a fantasy setting...."

Bruce lifted his hand to stop his tech from shifting into panic mode and pulling the plug. "No, not the Paris Experience. I'm going on a werewolf adventure. I have some friends who did a murder-mystery thing in Paris and loved it."

"Oh, cool." The tech put down the tablet with a relieved expression. "Yeah, Paris is a trendy setting for established couples. 'The City of Love' and all that. I did that one with a co-worker when it was in Beta."

God, the last thing Bruce wanted was to get whisked into something romantic and intimate where he was set up to fail, something that would remind him of all the ways Carrie said he sucked as a partner.

"I'm hoping for something very different," he said a little dryly.

The tech laughed. "Well, you're definitely getting that. You got paired to a custom scenario, which is super cool. Most people choose one of the premade adventures and request modifications, but this one was built from scratch."

Damn, that sounded like he'd gotten a treat without paying extra for it. Whoever he was partnered with for this was quite creative.

I wonder if she likes music...no, stop it!

"Does it cost more to create a custom Experience?"

"Not if the creator is willing to share the environment and doesn't claim exclusive rights to it. Don't ask how much they charge those who want to keep their environments private. Usually, executives from the big studios want to test out a movie idea, or the super-duper rich."

Bruce frowned. "I thought the Experience was supposed to be very private."

"It is." The tech smiled. "Think of your friends that had the Paris Experience. They will share the virtual city's backdrop with other couples, but not the details of their particular adventure."

Bruce let out a breath. "Got it."

"One more thing." The tech regarded him with a slight smirk, lifting the left corner of his lips. "I'm not supposed to give you any clues, but you indicated in the questionnaire that you would be open to other shifted forms. You might not be a werewolf."

"Yeah, yeah." Bruce waved a dismissive hand. "A jaguar, a lion, or even a bear is fine. What else is there?" His eyes widened as he remembered one adventure he'd passed over so quickly that he'd almost forgotten about it. "Oh, God. Please don't tell me I'm going to be a merman. Anything but a fish."

The tech laughed. "You're not going to be a merman, although it's an awesome adventure. I've done it a couple of times."

"I'll take your word for it."

"To each his own." Brian grabbed his tablet. "Are you ready to get started?"

"Yes."

"Let me run down the checklist real quick...yeah... yeah...mmhmm...oh, right!" He tapped the screen. "Did you choose a name for your avatar?"

"Bruce is fine." He shifted on the chair. "If it's good enough for Batman, it's good enough for a werewolf or anything else I might end up as. Is there a problem with using my name for my avatar?"

"Not at all. I just had to double-check that you

didn't misunderstand." The tech made some notation on his tablet. "Okay, Bruce. Close your eyes and relax. Don't fight it; just let yourself drift off to sleep, and you'll be in a new world when you wake up."

Bruce inhaled deeply and closed his eyes. It was going to be okay. This would be fun, a way to go anywhere without even leaving the city, and to move on from the things holding him in the past.

It was going to be grea...real gre...

10

KING BRUCE

*S*econds before the rising sun's first light pierced the horizon, Bruce stepped out onto his balcony and waited for the change that would transform him from an average-sized male into an enormous dragon.

Decades of practice had made him so attuned to the glowing orb in the sky that his body knew when it was time to wake up and leave the bed, no matter what time he'd gone to sleep. The one instance he had overslept and hadn't stepped out of his royal suite in time, he'd destroyed his rooms when the change occurred.

He'd never made the mistake of oversleeping again.

Thankfully, one of the perks of his curse of immortality was that he didn't need a lot of shut-eye or he wouldn't have had enough hours in the night to run his kingdom.

Shedding his robe, Bruce stood nude on the cold stone, and as goosebumps prickled his skin, he savored the sensation with appreciation. In a few seconds, he wouldn't be able to feel the chill or any of the hundreds of small sensations that his human body enjoyed. But until the first stirrings of the change robbed him of his humanity, he flexed his fingers, crunched his toes, and rolled his head from side to side.

It didn't take long.

The distant line of purple at the edge of the world turned red, then gold, and a second later, the light streamed out to touch the castle. Bruce moved forward as soon as he felt the faint warmth of it, taking a running step onto the balustrade and leaping off it without a care for the distant stone-covered square far below him.

For a moment, he fell unfettered, just a body plummeting toward the ground. It was terrifying, but something about it made Bruce feel so free.

A second later, the change took hold. In a burst of magic and a brief penetrating moment of pure expansion, Bruce transformed into the shape that had been his constant companion for the past forty years.

Wings unfolded with a crack, carrying him into the sky. Bruce pumped them steadily to soar high enough to see all of Ashelvin, the capital city of Trieste.

As his reptilian eyes scanned the ground, he

spotted no fires, no telltale signs of spell-casting, and no battles beyond a few drunken brawls.

Excellent.

Casting one final look back at the castle that had been his home for longer than his own father had lived in it, the Dragon King sped to the nearest border.

It had been many years since the sight of a huge cobalt-winged monster flying through the skies had been a cause for alarm. By now, every Trieste citizen was used to seeing their grumpy king patrolling the sky and keeping them safe.

As long as he kept their enemies at bay, his people didn't mind his fiery temper or gruff demeanor. They understood and accepted him the way he was.

After all, Bruce had come of age in a time of war, had lost nearly his entire family to it, and had gambled his own life in exchange for the lives of his people.

Most of them were grateful, and those who were not could leave. They didn't deserve to live inside the safe borders of Trieste and enjoy the protection of their king.

Thanks to him, they would be safe wherever they lived.

Since Bruce had made his dark bargain and defeated all of Trieste's enemies, none of their neighbors had attempted another incursion into his borders, and they hardly even bothered each other.

So yeah, he might not be the most popular

monarch around, and parents might use his fearsome reputation to scare their children into obedience, but Bruce didn't mind. There would be no senseless deaths on his watch, and for that, he was grateful to the damn witch.

She might have robbed him of a chance of ever finding love or becoming a father, but she'd made it so families all over the region could sleep in peace at night, and children didn't lose their fathers to wars their monarchs started out of boredom.

Wars were prevented because the other royals shook in their boots with fear at the mere mention of the Dragon King's name, and as a side benefit, they also refrained from throwing their daughters at him as potential brides.

The bards could wax poetic about love, but Bruce had no use for it. Love was just a weakness for others to exploit.

The dragon voiced his agreement with a fierce roar, but the human inside shook his head.

Think of your parents, your brother, and his wife before they died. Their love was a tender, warm thing, a way of supporting each other through the toughest of trials.

It was true, but how useful was that love in the end?

The need to protect their loved ones had just driven them to greater heights of heroism and self-sacrifice until it ended, inevitably, in death.

You would have done the same. You would have given

Rozia your life to protect your people. Instead, she only demanded your firstborn. You should count yourself lucky.

Yeah, he was lucky and didn't even mean it sarcastically.

His life was not about him but about serving his people.

Bruce was no longer the soft-hearted prince he'd been before the witch's magic had changed him in more ways than one. He was no longer the naive young man who had dreamt about falling in love and raising a family. Four decades later, only a handful of people remained who had known him as that man.

Most knew him as the grouchy, easily irritated dragon who roared at the sky and ruled his kingdom fairly but sternly.

His people knew better than to cross him or even bother him with trivialities. Just last night, he'd ordered that some quarreling farmers be thrown out of his reception hall. They were lucky that he hadn't been in his dragon form or he would have roasted them there and then.

He had no patience with petty disagreements between neighbors.

Hell, according to the dwindling palace staff, he had no patience at all.

11

KING BRUCE

*B*ruce landed heavily in the clearing designated for his use beside the first watchtower on his tour, which was on the border with Glorian.

A warlike nation once upon a time, Glorian had been the first to declare war. Now their king had all but abandoned the hundred miles of land they shared, but this was always the first place Bruce checked on each morning.

"Your Majesty." The Captain of the Guard strode out to meet him and bowed low.

Despite the early hour, the man's armor gleamed in the morning sun, and his surcoat was clean and hanging straight. The guy took his work seriously, which Bruce appreciated.

"Well met, Captain Hale." Bruce worked to keep his rumbling voice down.

The guards' horses were trained not to panic upon hearing him. Still, on more than one occasion, he'd sent entire herds of livestock into a frantic stampede. The shepherds in the area should know better than to try their luck in the rich pastureland in the nearby valley, at least not in the mornings.

"Report," he rumbled.

"Nothing of note happened last night," Captain Hale replied. "As you requested, I've compiled a weekly report from the other towers on this front. Would you like to read it yourself, or shall I summarize it?"

How was he supposed to read it in his dragon form? Hold the paper in front of his face speared on a talon?

"Summarize it for me, please. I don't have a lot of time."

"Of course, my liege." The captain bowed again. "Four out of the five towers reported zero incidents. The tower near Hariston has been dealing with nuisance incidents from local nobles, but it is nothing you should concern yourself with. The young men were just horsing around."

The nobles might be testing his zero-tolerance policy. It was better to respond quickly and quench the embers before they ignited the fire.

"Define nuisance," Bruce ordered.

The captain sighed. "They get drunk and throw rocks at the watchtower. The guards respond by arming the ballistae with water and giving the brats a good drenching, but they keep coming back."

Bruce huffed out an irritated breath.

Hariston had survived relatively well during the war thanks to its hilly terrain and isolated location, but the truth was that the war had ended a long time ago, and the new brood of Glorian nobles had no memory of the sound of screams or the scent of blood, which made them stupidly bold.

The Glorians were known as hotheaded people, and the young aristocrats had no outlet for their innate aggression, so they took it out on his watch tower.

He needed to show those beardless jackasses how unwise it was to tempt fate by aggravating the Dragon King.

"It's been too long since I stopped at that watch-tower," Bruce said. "I'll remedy that today."

Hariston was on the far end of the Glorian border, and the flight would take close to an hour. Still, it was time well spent if it served to remind the little cretins not to make trouble.

"I hope it won't delay you too long, sire." The captain smiled. "I just wish I could be there to see them running off with their tails between their legs."

Bruce cracked a rare smile in response, or at least he hoped that was what the dragon's expression conveyed. He could have looked as if he wanted to use the captain as a toothpick.

The guy didn't look alarmed, though, so perhaps the dragon managed to convey amusement.

"Anything else?" Bruce asked.

Captain Hale firmed his jaw. "A request, sire, from the local witches' guild. They want permission to harvest herbs here again. They say there's a particular blend of night-blooming marigold that—"

"No."

"Your Majesty, they're quite insistent about the good they'd be able to do for people if they had enough of the herb."

If Bruce's dragon face could sneer, it would be doing so right now. "I'm sure they are. They'll do so much good for the little people who come to them in exchange for giving away their futures and their children's. The answer is no, captain. It is 'no' right now, it will be 'no' tomorrow, and it is 'no' forever. None of them will get anything from me or the lands over which I hold sway."

What did witches care for the common good?

Nothing.

Not one of them had volunteered to use their magic to help defend Trieste during the war, not one of them had helped heal the sick or wounded, and the only one who had even bothered to meet with Bruce had ended up trying to force him into a bargain he could never accept.

None of them had been willing to help him find a way out of the deal either, no matter how unfair it was or what riches he had promised to the witch that would free him from Rozia's curse.

To hell with them.

The witches could roam the hills and forests for their potion ingredients like the scavengers they were. He wasn't going to make life easier for them.

He still held out hope that there was a way out of his plight, but he would find it without the witches' help.

Captain Hale bowed formally. "Understood. I'll make your will known to them, my liege."

"Carefully, captain," Bruce added. "Witches are spiteful and vindictive, and they don't react well to being denied."

He didn't want to see one of his best commanders turned into a newt or something worse for giving the witches' guild bad news.

"Careful is my middle name, sire."

Bruce huffed a low, dragonish laugh. "See that it is. I'll head to Hariston now. If I can't scare some sense into these young buffoons, nothing will."

"As you say, sire." Bruce began to work his wings as soon as Captain Hale was back by the watchtower.

Taking off from the ground was harder than throwing himself off a balcony—his dragon form was heavy, and on dry, dusty days, he could kick up quite a whirlwind during takeoffs. But this morning was mild, the grass dewy and green, and in the end, all he left behind were a few gouges in the turf and some bent sunflowers as he got airborne. He found a thermal current and let the rising heat carry him higher, then turned north toward Hariston.

He had some fools to intimidate.

CHARLOTTE

"*O*ut of the way, woman!" yelled the coachman.

Charlotte threw herself to the side of the road just in time to avoid being trampled by the lead horse of a quartet hauling a very ornate, undoubtedly very heavy, carriage behind them.

Through the window, she caught a glimpse of a bejeweled woman with a disinterested expression on her carefully made-up face. Preoccupied by the sight, Charlotte hadn't jumped far enough away, and as the carriage rolled by, its wheels kicked up a spray of mud and other unmentionables that the street was coated in, leaving a foul brown patina on the bottom of her best dress.

"Oh, hells," she muttered, glaring down at the stain with dismay.

Usually, she was so good at jumping out of the way

in time to avoid getting splattered, but today of all days she'd been too distracted to react fast enough. How was she going to present herself at the palace smelling like horse manure?

"Ah, lass," one of the vendors on the side of the road said with a chuckle. "New to Ashelvin, are you?"

With a sigh, she trudged over to her, the weight of the bag on her back suddenly feeling like too much. "Am I that obvious?"

"Apart from the kit you're carrying?" The woman smiled. "Everyone here knows it's better to walk on the side of the road and not in the middle where you can get trampled by a carriage."

She was standing behind a small cart, roasting pine nuts and stowing them in little paper sachets. The food smelled divine, but Charlotte couldn't think about the hole in her stomach right now.

"But it's so messy along the sides," she said, looking at the layer of muck she was now standing in. The closer to the middle of the road you were, the cleaner the path was.

Shit, as the saying went, rolled downhill.

"You need boot covers." The woman lifted one of her feet. She was wearing a pair of the thick, clunky leather-and-wood boots that had seemed ubiquitous to Charlotte since her arrival in the capital last night. "These are easy to clean but roomy enough to stick your regular shoes inside for entering an inn or the like." She slipped her foot out, and sure enough, she was wearing a pair of rather lovely red slippers.

"Oh, that makes sense." No wonder the shoe rack at the inn had been so full. Charlotte smiled apologetically at the woman. "I need to find some of those, I suppose. I'm from a much smaller town."

"The scholars' center in Glaeve, I expect."

For the second time in as many minutes, Charlotte was dumbfounded. "How did you know?"

The woman laughed again. It wasn't a mean laugh, thankfully, but Charlotte still blushed. "Oh, lass, you all come here looking the same! The purple hems, the massive ruck on your back, the wide eyes. It's clear as day where you're from. And in your case..." She looked Charlotte over for a moment. "I'm guessing you're a translator. That or a scribe."

"I..." Gods above, was everyone in this city going to find her so transparent? "I'm a scribe," she said faintly.

"Ah, so I thought. And don't worry there, lass." The woman gave her a wink. "I have a leg up when spotting the likes of you. My son is studying in Glaeve, so I know the look well."

"Oh." That made her feel better. Heartened at finding what seemed like the first friendly ear since her arrival, she decided to ask for help. "Do you know of a place where I might find some clean water? I can't present myself at the castle like this."

The woman's eyes widened. "The castle? What

happened? Has the last court scribe given up his job already?"

"Um...yes?"

"And they sent for you to take his place?" The woman looked incredulous.

Charlotte straightened her back. "I can do the work," she said stiffly.

"Oh, no, I don't mean to imply that you're incapable of doing the work," the vendor said, stirring the pine nuts absently. "I'm sure you can. It's just that the court scribe has to be around the king for many hours each day of the week."

"Naturally, that's the scribe's job." Charlotte could hardly be a court scribe and avoid spending time in the king's presence. "What of it?"

"Well, the king is known to be impatient. I don't know if you've heard, but he can be rather...ah. Abrupt."

"Oh, that." Now it was Charlotte's turn to laugh. "I can handle abruptness, mistress." *And rudeness, shouting, and all the other things I daresay you're unwilling to tell me.*

The woman sighed and shrugged her shoulders. "If you say so, lass. And yes, you can clean yourself up in my home." She called out behind her, "Daveth!"

As a young boy of nine or ten ran out of the building a moment later, she handed him the stirring spoon. "Mind the stall while I help Miss...."

"Cantref," Charlotte said. "Charlotte Cantref."

"Lovely to meet you, Miss Cantref. I'm Mistress Avies to my customers, but you can call me Pol." She motioned at the door of her house. "Come, come. You have plenty of time before presenting yourself to the king. It's not even three in the afternoon yet."

Charlotte frowned. "Is he not in court during the day?"

"You know of his curse, don't you?"

"I know he's a dragon, but he was cursed decades ago. Surely he's changed the castle enough to accommodate his new form?"

"Not our king," Pol said wryly as she led the way up the rickety steps, stopping to take her boots off by the door.

Charlotte winced at the sight of her shoes and did the same.

"He's as stubborn as a mule, that one. Won't allow changes to the castle, as he says it's only a matter of time before he's beaten the curse."

"Oh. Is that even possible?" Charlotte followed Pol into the narrow, dark house, turning slightly to get through the doorway with her pack on.

Pol sighed. "If it was, I think he would have found the cure long ago, poor man." She assumed a cheerier demeanor. "But enough of gossip! Come, I've got some hot water left from breakfast this morning. Let's get you cleaned up and off to the castle looking good as new. I've even got a pair of boot covers you can borrow to get you there."

"Thank you so much," Charlotte said.

"You can repay me with stories of Glaeve. My son is the worst at remembering to write to his poor mum, who misses him so badly and cherishes every letter he sends her." Pol pouted.

Charlotte smiled. "Deal."

CHARLOTTE

A few hours later, Charlotte approached the castle's front gate, clean, fed, and in a much better mindset. Feeling good about her prospects, she smiled at the gate guard. He smiled back reflexively before schooling his face into an impassive mask.

Despite the hour, the line of petitioners waiting to get in stretched across the courtyard, and since there was only one entrance Charlotte had no choice but to take a place in the line and wait her turn.

With so many people, it could take hours, and the straps of her rucksack were cutting into her armpits. Her pack was heavy, and although the weight sat comfortably on her hips for the most part, she wasn't sad to get a break from hauling her worldly possessions around. Taking it off, she laid it on the ground leaning against her leg and stretched her aching arms and back with a loud groan.

Her arrival at the capital hadn't been what she had envisioned. Still, thanks to the kindness of strangers, she'd managed to get where she needed to be despite the poor instructions she'd been given.

Just go to the palace and present your letter to the chamberlain.

Easy peasy. Right. No one told her where to find the chamberlain or what he looked like.

Bending to touch her toes with another appreciative groan, she admired the hedge of rose bushes that brightened the otherwise grey milieu. The castle could use some sprucing up.

"Excuse me, Miss," a male voice said behind her.

Since no one knew her, the man was probably addressing someone else.

Maybe in addition to the roses, the gardeners should plant petunias. They came in so many colors—

"Miss! I'm talking to you."

Charlotte frowned. Could he be addressing her after all?

She was still in the middle of her stretch, and as she turned her head, strands of hair fell to obscure her view. She brushed them aside only to see a very shiny pair of boots. Moving her gaze upward, she saw a pair of long legs clad in elegant breeches, then a matching vest that was half obscured by a big gold necklace.

Wait, that wasn't a necklace. It was actually a bunch of keys hanging from a gold chain.

Oh no! It was him! The chamberlain!

Charlotte straightened out of her stretch so fast that the blood rushed out of her head, leaving her dizzy. She would have fallen over if the chamberlain hadn't grabbed her arm, helping to hold her upright as she came back to herself.

It was positively mortifying.

"Miss Cantref, I presume," he said in a brisk tone once he was sure that she was capable of standing on her own.

How did he know who she was?

Her cloak gave her occupation away, but surely she wasn't the only scribe in the entire city.

"Yes, milord." Charlotte managed a curtsy.

"Excellent. I was wondering if you would ever arrive. I expected you yesterday."

"Ah." She felt her cheeks fill up with all the blood missing after her stretch. "I wasn't told that I needed to arrive at a certain time, but I would have been here yesterday if the wagon I was riding hadn't lost a wheel on the second day of my journey. It took a long time to fabricate a new one."

"I see. Well, no matter." The chamberlain gave her a brief, impersonal smile. "You're here now, and that's what counts. Come with me."

He waited impatiently for Charlotte to pick up her pack, then set off at a rapid pace through the castle courtyard, heading for one of the doorways.

It led into a hallway with large windows and torch sconces every twenty feet or so. Marveling at the smoothness of the marble beneath her feet, Charlotte was astounded by the luxury.

The bunting above the windows, likely ready to be dropped down at night to make curtains and keep the heat in, was gorgeous too. The thick cloth was embroidered with gold thread along the edges.

The scholars' center was financed by the crown, but the budget was modest, and the administration preferred to spend it on books and supplies. The facilities needed to be more robust at best and rough at worst, and the resident scholars lived no better than monks.

"It's high time the center provided us with a replacement," the chamberlain said. "Our last scribe left over a month ago and I made the request immediately following his departure."

"A month?" Heavens, that was a long time. "I don't know why it took them so long to send another scribe here, milord. There was no shortage of graduates waiting for suitable positions. I only just graduated last week, and I was overjoyed to receive a post so quickly and in service to the king, no less. It's such a great honor to work at the palace."

The chamberlain gave her a critical once-over. "I'm glad you're so enthusiastic, but I should warn you that the workload is heavy, and I doubt that an inexperienced scribe like you can handle it and the king's impatience. Recording the petitions and keeping track of the king's meetings is very challenging."

"I can do it, sir," Charlotte said confidently. She was a quick hand with a pen and excellent at notation, which allowed her to fulsomely fill in the events of a particular meeting at a later point. "I expected employment in one of the guilds and trained for speed accordingly."

"Mmm, yes. Speed will certainly help you, but it's not the key to succeeding at your new position."

Charlotte frowned. "It is not? Then what is?"

The chamberlain stopped and looked her in the eyes. "Dedication to your king," he said bluntly. "No matter how frustrated or frightened you might find yourself, you need to remain dedicated to doing your best to advance the king's mission and satisfy his wishes. This is not a position for the flighty or faint of heart, Miss Cantref. If you are prone to nerves or fits of hysteria, best tell me now and save us all the trouble of trying to integrate you into the workings of the court."

Nerves? Hysteria? What on earth was he talking about?

"I'm not prone to either of those things." Charlotte jutted out her chin. "I'm known as levelheaded and as someone who works well under pressure. Perhaps that's the reason Mistress Serafina chose me for the position. She knew I could handle it."

"Very well." The chamberlain nodded and began walking again.

CHARLOTTE

*C*harlotte tried to keep up with the chamberlain's long stride, which was difficult in her borrowed boots and the heavy rucksack on her back, but after the speech she'd given him about how capable she was, asking him to slow down was out of the question.

He turned into a smaller hallway with a green circle engraved above its entry and stopped in front of the third door.

"This is your room." He took a key from the ring around his neck, stuck it in the lock, and opened it up. Still standing in the corridor, he motioned for her to enter and didn't follow her inside.

It was the gentlemanly thing to do, and Charlotte appreciated it.

Taking her rucksack off, she set it down and looked around. The room's furnishings consisted of a single bed that was made up with freshly washed sheets, judging from the lavender smell. There was a small table, a candle holder, and a wardrobe for her things with a tiny mirror in it. There was even a desk and a narrow chair for her to work at.

It was very congenial, so much nicer than what she'd had in Glaeve.

Charlotte smiled with pleasure. "I love it!"

"Good. Come along, then." He waved his hand impatiently. "There is still more I need to show you, and I'm short on time."

She'd hoped to have time to unpack, but at least she wouldn't have to carry the sack, and clunk and click around the palace in her borrowed boots.

"Just a moment." She quickly removed them, straightened her robe, and glanced at the mirror to smooth her hair. An impatient huff from the chamberlain stopped her from fussing further with her appearance.

Evidently, he didn't care how she looked, and hopefully neither would the rest of the staff.

As soon as Charlotte rushed out of the room, the chamberlain relocked the door and handed her the key. "See that you don't lose it," he told her sternly.

"I won't." Charlotte put it in her pocket and scurried after the chamberlain as he led her down yet another hallway with windows that looked into the courtyard.

"Everything marked with a green circle indicates

that it is a staff and servants area, of which you are now a member." He pointed at a discreet symbol carved above the door. "This is our dining hall. Meals are served at seven in the morning, noon, five in the evening, and midnight. You can also find things to snack on at any time of the day or night."

Charlotte wrinkled her brow. "Midnight? Why would a meal be served at midnight?"

"Everything in the castle runs according to the king's schedule."

"But why would he eat at midnight?"

The chamberlain turned an exasperated look at her. "I am sure you are aware that King Bruce is a dragon from sunrise to sunset and a man from sunset to sunrise."

"Yes, of course. Everyone knows that."

He gave her a look that implied he was questioning her intelligence.

"In what form do you think he hears most of his petitions?"

"As a man?"

"And when is our king a man?"

"After sundown," she murmured. "I just didn't realize he had to work so late at night."

The truth was that she hadn't even thought of that at all.

Over the years, she'd seen the king many times in his dragon form, flying over the cities of Trieste, watching out for danger or trouble. He'd even helped put out a fire in the scholars' center once, smothering the flames that had burst out from the kitchen building with heavy beats from his wing. Charlotte had been just fifteen then, new to the center, and seeing the king up close had awed her, leaving her with a sense of gratitude and wonder and a little sadness. The Dragon King couldn't even enter the structure in his huge form after saving it. He would have had to wait for nightfall, but then he couldn't have returned to the palace swiftly by flying over the land.

The chamberlain let out a breath. "Bravo. Perhaps you are a scholar, after all."

His tone was sarcastic, but Charlotte couldn't fault him for thinking she was daft. How come it had never occurred to her that the king couldn't hold court in his dragon form?

Ignoring the sarcastic comment, she smiled at the man. "Not a problem. It will take me a couple of days to adjust to sleeping while the sun is up and working when it's down, but I will manage."

The chamberlain snorted. "That is not going to be your schedule. You will make yourself available to the king whenever he has need of your services. He does occasionally handle court duties in his dragon form. In addition, he will need you to read to him the missives he receives from other courts and nobles."

Good grief, what else was she going to have to do, perform dances for the man?

"Why can't he read them himself?"

"As a man, he can, but how is he supposed to do so as a dragon?"

That was a good point. Each of the dragon's eyes was bigger than the standard size of missives. The small letters were probably illegible to him. Besides, how was he going to hold up the paper?

"Can't he wait to read them when he's a man?"

"Our king also has to sleep sometime, Miss Cantref." The chamberlain's voice had gone cold. "Our king works tirelessly to ensure the safety and prosperity of our kingdom and its people, and we need to help him in any way we can. If I could get him two scribes, or three, or a dozen to help make the work lighter, it would ease his workload and yours significantly, but after countless scribes have quit, the scholars' center is chary of providing their assistance. We have to make do with what we have."

She wondered why the king hadn't ordered the center to provide him with more scribes, but she'd already made a fool of herself and had lost some esteem in the chamberlain's eyes. She should find someone else to answer her questions.

"I'll do my best," she murmured under her breath.

The chamberlain finally slowed down and gave her a tight smile. "That's all any of us can do. Be prompt, be efficient, and try to be understanding. If you can survive a year, I will give you a glowing reference to get you a permanent post with any guild in the country."

Positions like that were rare as hens' teeth and scribes held on to them tightly. Even a letter of recommendation from the king's chamberlain couldn't guarantee that she would get one of those coveted jobs, but she would take it with both hands.

"Thank you." She dipped her head. "I'm not a quitter like those other scribes, and if it's up to me, I will survive as long as the king needs me. But what if I make a mistake?"

The king's bad temper was legendary, and if she had to work with him while he was in his dragon form, he might roast her in a fit of anger.

"Just apologize for it and move on. The king will...understand."

That hadn't sounded encouraging. She was bound to make mistakes in the beginning, to misunderstand and blunder. Perhaps, she should lock herself in her room when the king returned to his castle in his dragon form and wait until nightfall before making herself available to him. After they'd worked together for a while and he was happy with her services, she could expand it to daylight hours.

After all, it wouldn't do to get burnt to a crisp by an angry dragon during her first week at work.

Yes, that was undoubtedly the best plan. She nodded to the chamberlain. "Thank you for the advice, sir. I shall remember it."

He chuckled. "Thank me once you make it past your first day." He waved his hand. "Come. I'll show you where to do your laundry." He led her through a corridor overlooking the courtyard and the beautiful rose garden that looked even more magnificent from the third floor than it looked from the ground. "By the way, no one is allowed outside the castle half an hour before sunset and half an hour after that. All the doors will be locked, but in case someone is negligent and leaves one open, don't get tempted to venture outside. The king is particularly grumpy when he returns from his patrols, and he needs this hour of solitude among his beloved roses."

15

KING BRUCE

Worthless, stinking, petty, ridiculous little shits.

The trip to Hariston to scare some sense into the stone throwers had quickly devolved into an outcry by the town across the border, and the young lord in charge of the place had ridden out, plate armor gleaming as only unused armor could, and demanded that Bruce apologize for flying over land that didn't belong to him.

"An incursion that will not be tolerated," the lordling called from the safety of his horse a thousand feet away from the border.

The only way he could project his voice like that was with the help of a witch.

Bruce wasn't fond of witches to begin with, and certainly not when they used their magic to help stir up trouble, which they seemed to revel in.

Stepping across the border, or rather stomping over it, he stood well inside Glorian territory.

"What about this?" he rumbled, anger making his voice even more gravelly than usual. "What do you call it when I stand on your ground with my own four feet, hmm?"

As he stalked right up to the lord, and the guy's horse scented the approaching beast, the animal bucked his master right off and galloped away, leaving the little fool flat on the ground, staring up at Bruce with an expression of horror on his unlined face.

"You can call it one of two things," Bruce went on. "If this is an incursion, then that means we're at war. If we're at war, then I'll treat you as my enemy and bite you in half right here and now."

The lord whimpered, and the sharp stench of urine rose from his chainmail trousers.

"However—" Bruce leaned over the terrified lord. "If this is merely a friendly parley, then there is no trouble between our two countries, and we can talk about the unacceptable actions of a few unruly young men who need to be taught a lesson with no need for a fight. The choice is yours."

"P-p-parley," the lord got out. "I choose parley! Of course, just a parley, not a...not an incursion. It was just a poor choice of words born from inexperience. Please, forgive me."

"Indeed." Bruce leaned back enough to give the lord some breathing room so he could get to his feet and attempt to salvage his dignity. "Let's discuss the measures you will take to stop these youths from lobbing rocks at my tower."

"Childish diversions," the man insisted with a nervous titter of laughter. "I'll deal with them, and they will never throw rocks again."

"As long as the rock throwing stops, I'll never mention it again," Bruce agreed, and that was that.

Despite the peaceful resolution of the conflict, Bruce felt far from calm as he flew back to Ashelvin.

The incident had taken longer than he had expected, which meant that he had to rush through his route and then fly like the wind to make it to the castle before the transformation occurred and he dropped like a rock from the sky and got splattered on the ground below.

He was tired and irritated, which meant that the dragon was seething and releasing streams of fire and plumes of smoke on the way, scaring animals and people alike.

At least he'd managed not to fry anyone.

He hadn't had to push himself like that in over a decade, and he was exhausted by the time he finally landed in the castle courtyard with mere moments to spare.

As per his instructions, the place was vacant at this time of day. The magic of his transformation wasn't pretty, probably made so on purpose by the hateful witch, and no one needed to hear the awful sounds that occurred as his body folded itself from dragon form to human in seconds.

Regrettably, he was too big and heavy in his dragon form to land on his bedroom's balcony or anywhere else in the structure. He'd once tried to land on one of the towers, and the whole thing crumbled, miraculously not killing anyone.

The only area of the palace large enough and safe for him to land was the front courtyard.

Bruce was used to the sound of cracking bones by now, and the pain barely registered anymore, but it was a terrifying sight to behold.

Once human again, he staggered over to the bench set for him right between the rose bushes and pulled out the suit of clothes and food that had been left for him under it. After getting dressed, he opened the food basket and devoured half a roasted chicken and two rolls in minutes.

Feeding himself as a dragon was problematic, to say the least, and Bruce had learned the hard way that it was far better to sate himself in his human form than to try to satisfy his dragon's stomach, because that took an entire flock of sheep and left behind very unhappy shepherds.

It was only once he'd started in on the dessert that he detected a tiny rustling sound nearby, almost like the movement of a small animal, but since no creatures would voluntarily get close to him in either form, it had to be one of the palace staff or an assassin.

If it was some new recruit feeling brave and making a daring wager with his friends to get near the Dragon King when he wasn't supposed to, Bruce was going to scare the living daylights out of him.

But if it was an assassin, he would show him no mercy.

It had been a very long time since anyone had attempted to catch him in his human form to try to kill him when they thought it would be easier. They hadn't succeeded then, and they wouldn't now.

The palace had been protected from witchcraft since the day it was built centuries ago, so assassins couldn't use magic to help them, and no un-enhanced mortal was strong enough or fast enough to kill Bruce in either of his forms.

Dropping the plate, he whirled around, automatically reaching for the sword that had been left along with the clothes and pulling it out of the scabbard.

"Who's there?" he demanded harshly. "Show yourself, worm!"

"Ah..." There was a shuffle, a slight rustling of the rose bush, and then out from behind it stepped a young woman in scribe's garb, with rose-gold hair packed into a disheveled braid and a mortified expression on her heart-shaped face.

She could have been pretty if her sweet face wasn't contorted in fear.

Maybe if he put the sword down...

But what if she was an assassin?

The thought was so ridiculous that Bruce had to force himself not to laugh.

"Who are you?" He laid the sword on the bench, leaving it within easy reach.

It was better to be safe than sorry, as his mother used to say.

"I'm—I'm a—a scribe, and—your scribe, I mean. Your new scribe, and I—um—"

She was going to babble herself breathless at this rate.

"I can tell you are a scribe from your clothing. I want to know who you are, what's your name, and what you are doing hiding among my rose bushes at a time when no one is supposed to be out here."

She squeaked, her back stiffening so hard it was a wonder her poor spine didn't break. "I'm so sorry! My name is Charlotte, Charlotte Cantref, and I—well, I just arrived today. I was being shown around by your chamberlain, and it was right after dinner, and I thought it might be nice to have a few roses to put up in my new room to liven it up a little. Not that it isn't already lovely! It's so nice, better than what I had at the scholars' center, certainly, but a flower never goes amiss, does it? So, I figured I would pick a rose, but there are so many lovely colors and scents that I got lost, and I sort of forgot about the sunset because, well..." She chuckled weakly. "Castle walls. I can't actually see the sunset. And then I remembered and tried to leave because I knew you would be coming back, but all the doors in the courtyard were already locked, and no one came when I pounded on them, so I just decided to hide and...and hope for the best."

"That was your plan?" Bruce asked flatly. "Hope for the best?"

Did she know who her king was? Had she heard of his temper and what he did to those who disregarded his wishes?

How hard was it to give him the one hour of privacy he demanded?

The young woman—Charlotte—flushed. "I didn't mean to disturb you, my king. It was an accident." She bowed her head. "I should have been more careful, and I promise not to do it in the future, but really it's my first day, and you could try to be a little more understanding."

"More...understanding?"

Was he actually hearing what he thought he was hearing?

The imp was trying to justify her intrusion into what should have been time just for him, a time he had fought to carve out in his life of service and dedication over the past four decades, a moment when he could be vulnerable without having to worry about putting up a front for the people who lived in his castle and served his will?

This moment was the closest thing he had to something sacred, and today it had been violated by an impudent scribe.

He drew in a breath and opened his mouth to begin yelling at her and just as abruptly closed it.

You need a scribe. Desperately.

He had people who could do the work but not as fast, and he refused to borrow someone from the guilds when the scholars' center had damn well been promising him another scribe after the last one had lost his nerve a week into his service.

And why did that happen?

Because Bruce had lost his temper, just like he was a hair away from losing it now.

Look at her; she's too delicate to take a verbal drubbing and return. Unless you want to keep your staff by dint of tyranny instead of loyalty, you must control your angry outbursts.

Bruce noticed how white the knuckles of Charlotte's hands were where they were clenched in front of her waist, and the minute trembles that shook her shoulders. If he laid into her now, he might not get another chance of a scribe for a year.

"Very well," he said at last. "I will let it slide this once because you are new to the place, and I will even pretend to accept the apology you didn't make."

"Oh! I'm so sorry—"

"Oren!" he bellowed, ignoring her belated attempt to appease him.

Not ten seconds later, one of the doors into the

courtyard opened, and his chamberlain came in at a pace so brisk it was practically a run.

"Sire," he said, bowing low once he came to a stop. "I beg your forgiveness for this breach of protocol. Miss Cantref is new to the castle, and I should have impressed upon her how important this private hour is to you. I will take full responsibility for her actions."

That was more like it.

Oren was probably defending the girl because he didn't want them to lose another scribe, but he would have taken responsibility regardless of that.

Bruce didn't need his subjects to grovel before him, but he did need them to acknowledge their mistakes and try to do better. "See that it doesn't happen again," he said. "Get her whatever she needs to begin her work. I will open court in ten minutes." It was faster than he usually went, but Bruce was tired, and he wanted to be done for the day sooner than later. "How many petitioners do we have today?"

"As many as any other day, sire."

"Where are all the people who were lined up in here earlier?" Charlotte asked with no trace of fear remaining on her beautiful face.

Bruce smiled. He was going to enjoy watching her first court experience. "You'll soon see."

16

CHARLOTTE

*C*harlotte had expected the position of a court scribe to be a little more glamorous, but she was starting to realize that the Dragon King had little regard for luxuries. Everything in Bruce's court was kind of basic except for things that had remained from bygone eras of grandeur.

Getting ready for scribing consisted of being handed an enormous sheaf of paper, a substandard pen, and a bottle of watery ink. Her station in the throne room was a desk that seemed to be a relic from more glamorous days, and sitting behind it, Charlotte felt like she had when she'd sat at her father's desk as a young girl.

She'd written her parents about getting the position in the king's court. She was sure they were proud of her. Still, she had left the scholars' center before their return letter had arrived. She wondered whether anyone would think to forward the letter to the palace.

Besides, she had so much more to tell them, like how handsome the king was in his human form.

King Bruce could have been even more handsome if he had smiled once in a while and didn't frown as much, but it was understandable why he was so grumpy. Everyone knew about the war that had cost him his family, and the bargain with the witch that had cost him a normal life and a chance at happiness.

Bruce had been granted immortality, and he looked like a young man of twenty and some years, but his hair had gone completely gray from the sorrows he had endured.

Poor guy.

Charlotte wished she had a talent for amusing people like her friend Shanti did, so she could bring more smiles to the king's solemn face. But she was terrible at telling jokes, always bungling the delivery or the end, and she was even worse at impressions.

Could she convince Shanti to come work at the palace?

Nah. Her friend's family were big merchants, and Shanti was expected to come home and work in their business.

"You'll do your initial note-taking here," Oren said as she put her writing instruments on the enormous desk.

It was good to have a name for the man instead of

thinking of him as the chamberlain. But since he had yet to volunteer it, she should keep addressing him by his title.

"The king hears petitions and goes through his official correspondence for four hours in the evening of every day except for Sundays. Usually, that's enough time to get through it all, but on some days, it isn't, and you are expected to stay here with him until he tells you that you can go."

"Why didn't you mention this before?" Charlotte mumbled quietly as she readied her equipment.

She winced at the ink's poor quality, which would take forever to dry. No wonder the desk was so big— she would have to lay her sheets out for at least fifteen minutes before stacking them.

"I did," Oren said.

"You said I'd have to be available to the king when needed."

The chamberlain rolled his eyes. "For an intelligent woman, you sometimes act daft. I'll put it in simple terms—whenever the king needs a scribe, you're there, and it doesn't matter how long you've worked that day or what hour of the night it is. Consider this reparation for being privy to everything the king does. It's a singular privilege and requires great trust." He regarded her with a stern look. "I know that the scribe code demands that you never reveal the things you transcribe, but I'll reiterate. The surest way to get burned to a crisp is to betray the king's trust."

Charlotte shivered. "I'd never do that."

Gods above, seeing the Dragon King land a few feet away from her had been mortifying. He was so prominent in his other form, majestic and beautiful. As the dust settled from the impact of his enormous paws, she'd hidden in the bushes, so she hadn't seen the transformation, but the sounds alone had been terrifying—the groans and loud cracks—it must have been painful.

Did the king suffer agonizing pain twice every day, day in and day out?

Four decades of that would drive anyone mad.

Charlotte knew as much as the next person about the curse on their king, which wasn't a lot. No one knew if the witch had reneged on her part of the deal and refused to turn him back or if she had twisted it on him in some way like witches were known to do. When dealing with the witches, even under the auspices of their guild that provided their clients with some modicum of protection, one had to be extremely careful. Using an experienced scribe that was familiar with how witches conducted business might have saved Trieste's future king from making a terrible deal.

Then again, it might have been the prince who had failed to hold up his end of the agreement once his objective had been met.

People didn't cross witches and come out on top.

The people of Trieste were grateful to their king, and knowing he would be there to look after them perpetually was reassuring. Not knowing her monarch personally and not realizing the enormity of his sacrifice, Charlotte had felt like that until just an hour ago. Now, though, she felt sad and guilty for taking him for granted.

What a cruel fate.

When the king entered the throne room a few minutes later, she schooled her features to keep all signs of pity out of her expression. Before, when she'd seen him wearing simple linen pants and a shirt, which he must have donned right after his transformation, he could have been almost any well-built, broodily attractive man. But wearing his formal regalia, King Bruce cut an impressive figure.

Wearing a blue and gold doublet and trousers, high leather boots, a velvet cloak, and a gold and sapphire crown on his head, the randomly attractive man had become, most decidedly, the handsome but distant King Bruce.

The Dragon King.

Still, the image of him in the simple attire, which hadn't left much to the imagination, was what Charlotte saw every time she closed her eyes.

Gods above, why was she still thinking about how handsome her king was?

"Send in the first petitioner," King Bruce said.

No, she wasn't ready yet!

Charlotte hastily picked at the wax seal on the bottle of ink, trying to get enough of the crumbly stuff off to free the cork that was keeping it all contained. Whoever had sealed this bottle had probably spent more on the wax than the cheap ink inside.

Ugh, this was taking forever, and the doors were already open, the first petitioner stepping forward, and she was trying to work as quickly as possible without drawing attention to herself. Still, the damn cork was stuck, and maybe if she stuck it between her knees, she might—*pop*!

The bottle opened so abruptly that Charlotte lost her grip, and half the contents flew out over her official dress before she managed to right the bottle.

"Damn it," she muttered, looking at the mess in her lap. She needed to change before the ink set in, and—

She was halfway to her feet when she realized King Bruce was staring at her. "Where do you think you're going?" he asked.

Oh, hells. "I...there was a little accident with the ink," Charlotte explained, gesturing down to her skirts as her cheeks heated with embarrassment. "I was just going to change. I'll come right back. Sire," she added belatedly.

"Absolutely not."

Wait, what?

Fortunately, the words didn't make it out of her mouth before King Bruce went on, "My people have been waiting all day to have their petitions heard. I won't have them wait longer over a bout of clumsiness. If there is ink left in the bottle, then the rest can wait."

Oh, it was all right for her to sit here, damp and humiliated, while the ink set so deeply into the fabric of her skirt that she could never get it out, all so the king could start his court a little sooner?

After flying around all day defending their nation and returning only to have his moment of solitude interrupted by another of Charlotte's miscalculations?

Well...when you put it like that...

"Yes, your Majesty," she said with almost no resentment before sitting back down and preparing her pen.

The nib was poorly trimmed, ensuring that her note-taking would be scratchy enough to be heard throughout the entire throne room.

Wonderful. Just fantastic.

She forced a smile onto her face. "I'm ready, sire."

17

KING BRUCE

*U*nder normal circumstances, or whatever passed for normal these days, Bruce wouldn't have been so harsh with his new scribe. At least, he liked to think he would have been more gracious.

Mistakes happened. He understood that.

Hell, his entire existence was the result of a massive mistake. Underestimating Rozia and letting his desperate need to stop the bloodshed and win the war overpower his common sense and better judgment had cost him dearly. Not a day had gone by without him thinking about all the things he could have done to outsmart the witch and prevent his situation.

Witches were known to be tricky, and he should have gone to see Rozia with others. He should have taken one of his father's wise advisors to make sure that every word of the deal he'd made was clearly articulated, leaving no room for loopholes for the witch to use later.

But he'd been young, impulsive, and desperate.

Still, Charlotte was about the same age he'd been back then, and if spilling the ink had been her only transgression, he would have let her go and change.

But it hadn't been. She'd intruded on his private moment, and Bruce wasn't above petty revenge.

He still felt...vulnerable.

No, not that. Kings weren't allowed to feel vulnerable, especially not kings who were also dragons. But he felt a bit off-kilter after being seen in a way he hadn't been ready for.

The fact that it had been an accident didn't change that. So, no changing for Charlotte. No pausing the proceedings. They had a lot to get through tonight, and they were going to do it no matter how uncomfortable either—or both—of them were.

His staff had ranked the petitioners earlier in the day, and Bruce handled the simplest cases first. The most interesting of those was an issue of property rights going to a daughter who had technically married 'out' of the family, making her male cousins think they could grab her father's store.

"This is ridiculous," Bruce said after hearing both sides make their complaints.

The young woman, accompanied by her husband and wearing blue and white mourning bands in memory of her father, hung her head defeatedly as her older cousins smiled triumphantly at each other.

The morons were in for an unpleasant surprise. They should have examined the law book before bringing their case to court.

Changing the inheritance laws was one of the first things Bruce did when he ascended to the throne.

"If any of you had worked in the store, helped build its reputation and clientele, you might have offered to buy your cousin out." Bruce glared at the men.

The woman looked up, a hopeful light on her face.

Off to the side, Charlotte was rapidly scratching away at the paper.

"But you did not," Bruce continued. "Instead, you relied on an obsolete law to prey on a grieving family member and demanded that she give you something her father spent his life building and that she is capably running right now."

"But she's married," one of the male cousins said.

Bruce turned and glanced at Oren. "Cite the law to enlighten this ignorant man."

"Section seven, subsection two," Oren said immediately. "Inheritance of any and all property is to be equally distributed between the male and female children of the deceased. Without direct descendants, it is to be equally distributed between the other relatives regardless of gender. This law has been in effect for thirty-seven years."

More than long enough for these morons to be aware of it.

Changing that particular law had been one of Bruce's proudest moments early in his reign. He was sure they knew about it but had thought to use the daughter's ignorance of it to cheat her out of her inheritance.

Luckily, she hadn't just accepted their claim and had brought it to court.

If the cousins had any brains between them, they would have let it go before coming to his throne room and risking his wrath.

"Case is dismissed." Bruce banged his staff on the floor. "The fact that your local magistrate even allowed it to get as far as my throne room is an insult."

One of the men blanched.

Ah, perhaps he was friends with that particular magistrate. Perhaps he'd hoped that Bruce wouldn't bother to hear a case like this in person and would simply put his seal on the lower official's decision.

Well, tough shit. "Write down his name," Bruce looked at Oren. "I'll be pursuing a review of all of his cases now." He waved at the group of petitioners still standing in front of his dais. "Dismissed."

The young woman and her relieved husband bowed low. "Thank you, your Majesty," she said, her cheeks running with grateful tears.

"You're welcome." Uncomfortable with both tears and gratitude, Bruce waved her out again. "Next case."

Once he was through with the local cases, he moved on to disputes between his nobles and guild issues. Some of these were represented by actual people, but most were read aloud by Oren. It was all fine, if somewhat boring, until—

"The healers' guild asks for your permission to work with the witches' guild in the pursuit of rare herbs that will allow them to increase their stock of medications in advance of—"

"No." Bruce's voice cut like a knife. Everyone in earshot stared at him in variations of surprise and terror, but he was too angry to heed their emotions.

The witches had already found a new way to hound him in less than a day. He had warned them not to look to him for leniency and understanding. Yet, lately, they just kept pushing, pushing, constantly pushing.

The witches knew very well what would gain them favor with him. Until they offered him release from the curse on a golden platter and with apologies from their guild mistress, they should expect nothing but scorn from him.

"Your Majesty," began Oren, ever the peacemaker. "Honoring this request wouldn't require any contact between you and the witches. It would simply make it easier for the healers to acquire the herbs they need to ensure the health and safety of our citizens."

"Something that they've been able to do very successfully on their own for countless years without the witches' help," Bruce snapped. "No. I will not condone a formal partnership between these guilds. No one is to aid the witches in any way."

"Sire—"

"Don't 'sire' me like you're trying to handle me," Bruce said, his fury rising. Oren ought to know better. "My answer is no, and that's final. If the head of the healers' guild takes issue with it, she can bring her complaints to me in person. Otherwise, my ruling is final."

He stood up fast, his cloak spreading around him like a pair of wings before settling again. "Court is over. You're all dismissed." He glanced at Charlotte, disliking the edge of fear in her wide eyes.

Apparently, he scared her no matter what form he took.

No one will ever know you.

No one will ever understand.

Why even wonder if it's possible?

Bitter and angry, Bruce pointed at the papers on her desk. "I expect those to be written formally and delivered to my rooms before sunrise."

"But...but it's already midnight!" she protested.

Was it?

No wonder he was so hungry.

"If you can't handle the work, then leave."

Whirling around, he walked out of the throne room and headed toward his suite, where he knew more food and a bath would await him. He might be able to catch a few hours' worth of sleep before he had to get up and start it all over again.

Except tomorrow, you'll be back to not having a scribe, you fool.

Bruce sighed, disappointed with himself but not truly surprised.

Even those who knew him best found him hard to deal with. How could he imagine that a greenhorn like Charlotte Cantref would do any better?

CHARLOTTE

*I*n the wake of the king's exit, the courtroom had gotten so quiet that a drop of water striking the stone floor would have sounded like thunder.

Oren, far from looking surprised, mainly seemed resigned. "Clear the room," he called out.

When the various functionaries and servants had left, he walked over to Charlotte's desk and shook his head. "I'm sorry that your first day of work has gone so poorly," he apologized.

"He really doesn't like witches, does he?" Charlotte asked faintly.

Her heart was still thundering, partly from anger and partly from fear.

King Bruce had gone from the slightly irritated but rational man she'd been witnessing for hours to someone completely different in the space of a moment.

Someone terrifying.

"He does not, no." Oren sighed. "I'd hoped that couching contact with them through a request from a guild he approves of would make it easier for him to bear, but that was my own naïveté. As for what he said to you," Oren gestured at the desk, "I understand if you're less enthusiastic about the position after this. I promised you a letter of recommendation after a year, but I might be able to—"

"No!"

Charlotte felt as surprised by her own outburst as Oren looked, but it was meant genuinely. "I'm not leaving," she said, clarifying it for him and herself. "It won't take nearly as long to transcribe the proceedings as he thinks, and I won't let him run me out on my first day." Or night. Whatever.

"It took the last scribe many hours to finish rewriting court documents," Oren said doubtfully. "How are you so sure you can do it faster?"

"Because I'm not rewriting anything," Charlotte said with a smile, her confidence returning now that they were talking about her area of expertise. "Your last scribe must have been very traditional. We've learned to leave space in the original document for the words that need to be added. The notations can be integrated right into the expanded text. It takes less than half the time." She pointed to the hash marks on the nearest paper, which, to many eyes, would look like nothing at all. To her, they were the shorthand script that would let her retell verbatim the tale of the king's refusal to consider the proposal of the healers' guild.

"Oh." Oren looked surprised. "That's very clever. Hmm...why did you protest against the king's desire to have the documents by dawn, then?"

Charlotte scoffed. "Because it's obvious he's just trying to make me feel overwhelmed. If he really needed these documents done tonight, he would have told me to have them done well before the hour that he turns back into a dragon. Right? I mean, you already told me he can't even read documents in his dragon form, so he wants them so fast because he's trying to nettle me." Just like with the ink and her ruined outfit.

"You're right," Oren said slowly, looking at her with an assessing eye. "Perhaps he's testing your mettle."

"Does he do this to all his new scribes?" Charlotte asked.

"No. In fact, he hardly pays them any attention at all. Over the years, King Bruce has concluded that the best way for his people to get their work done is for them not to be afraid of him looking over their shoulders. That's held true even with the scribes. Your predecessor quit because he was too put off by the workload to continue, not because our king ever paid him any special attention. But you..."

Charlotte eyed the chamberlain apprehensively. "But me what?"

Oren smiled. "Don't worry about it. Just be yourself. I think that's what the king needs more than anything."

"I don't know how to be anyone else," Charlotte pointed out.

"Well, you're still new to the court. You'll learn." Oren pointed at her dress. "Let's get you cleaned up, then discuss what you need so you can do your work here. I saw the look on your face when you picked up that ink," he added when Charlotte opened her mouth to protest. "You've got standards; the least I can do is ensure we meet them."

"Well...thank you." Charlotte stacked the papers in her arms, leaving the substandard ink and pen on the desk. "As it happens, I do have some idea of improvements that could be made to the process. I've absolutely got to use my own quill, for one, and I'll need to—"

"You can tell me about them as we walk to the laundry room."

Oh right. She might get there in time to save this outfit after all.

19

CHARLOTTE

*T*hree hours of filling in the blanks later, along with a break for a meal and several hot cups of tea, Charlotte had fulfilled King Bruce's directive.

Gallantly, Oren had kept her company until she was done, but when she tried to hand him the documents to deliver to the king, he shook his head. "You should deliver them yourself."

Her eyes widened. "He's most likely asleep. I think it's best to leave them by his door so that when he wakes up and finds them, he will know that I completed the task on time.

With a smile, Oren took her elbow and guided her down the dimly lit hall leading to the king's chambers. "If he's awake and has questions concerning what you've written, it's only appropriate that you are there to answer them."

"But what if he's asleep?" Charlotte winced. "I would hate to wake him up." *And be snarled at all over again.*

"King Bruce doesn't have a sleep schedule," Oren said. "If he's asleep, trust me, he won't wake up due to a few little taps on the door. If he's awake, however, he'll appreciate the chance to put his time to good use. There are so many things requiring his attention already. He will surely appreciate knocking a few off his list."

"If you say so, but if he snarls at me, I'll blame it on you."

"No problem. I'm used to his snarling." They stopped in front of the immense wooden door at the end of the hall carved with inlays of dragons and other mythical beasts. "Do it like this." Oren rapped once, firmly.

Charlotte waited tensely, half worried at the prospect of seeing the king again and half...excited?

Expectant?

She didn't quite know how to phrase it, but a part of her was looking forward to the experience. Goodness, when had she become a masochist?

After a minute with no reply, Oren nodded once, opened a slot in the door covered by a polished brass fitting, and pushed the papers through. "It's a shelf," he said when Charlotte made what had to be a horrified expression. "They're not just fanning out all over the floor, I assure you."

"Oh, I wasn't worried about that...much," she said sheepishly.

"I wouldn't be so careless with your work," he replied. "And neither would King Bruce. The documents are an essential part of the King's justice system. Without which there would be little protecting the citizenry from the powerful and the rich."

"Is it really?" she asked as they turned and began to walk away.

"Indeed. Our king is concerned with everyone in his kingdom, not just those with privilege." Oren's expression was a bit chagrined as he said, "If there is one good thing that's come of his transformation apart from keeping us safe, it's the fact that he's impossible to bribe. After all, what can anyone offer a man like King Bruce? The only thing he wants is a cure, and the witch responsible for his change is the only one who can give him that."

"And she won't?" Charlotte pressed, intrigued.

"I don't know the details," Oren demurred. "All I know is that after their last meeting, the king returned to the castle enraged like I've never seen him before, and that is saying something given that he's always angry. He forbids anyone who works here from having direct contact with any witch, and he won't allow them into Ashelvin. As you witnessed earlier tonight, he's still very set against working with them even in matters that would benefit the people."

"He must have a good reason for it," Charlotte said.

That wasn't a lie, either—Bruce didn't seem like the type of man to turn away from hard things just because he didn't like them.

"I'm sure he does," Oren agreed. They finally came to a stop outside Charlotte's room. "Get some rest," he advised her. "You did very well for your first night. If you sleep through the seven o'clock meal, more food will be available at noon."

"Thank you." Charlotte curtsied, then went inside and shut the door behind her with a huge sigh.

What a day. What a night. Sleep would be so good.

Still, she couldn't shake off her disappointment at not seeing the king one last time before heading to bed. Especially if he had been ready for bed and wearing a thin sleep shirt…

"Get over yourself, Charlotte." She sighed.

What the king looked like under his clothes was no business of hers. She wasn't a princess or even a noble. The king would never regard her as anything more than a servant.

20

KING BRUCE

*B*ruce sailed through the clear skies, high enough not to spook the herds of sheep and cattle that grazed far below him. Learning to catch a thermal and fly high had been one of the more complicated tricks to pick up after his initial transformation, but on a day like this, the skill was invaluable.

He hated to admit it, but he was…tired.

Tired, pah.

He was a king and a dragon. He didn't have time for tired! But he couldn't deny that lately, he hadn't been sleeping as well as he ought to, which was entirely the fault of the new scribe.

Well, no.

It was his own fault.

But damn it, if he couldn't be petty in the depths of his own mind, when could he be?

Perhaps he ought to hold himself to higher standards and transcend the impulse, but if he hadn't mastered that in his more than sixty years in this world, forty of them as king and dragon, he was probably destined to be frivolous for life.

After another court session, he'd spent nearly all night with his new scribe, which had been an exciting experience for sure, but he was now paying the price for that indulgence.

Charlotte was a strange combination of innocence and nearly arrogant confidence. She was the opposite of timid, speaking her mind like no one else around him dared, but she did her work diligently, so he couldn't complain about that, although he could complain about how it looked. It wasn't as neat as that of his former scribes, and having it all explained as a new style of scribing and something that everyone was using now was not good enough.

"Oh, is it, now?" he'd said, staring at the spacing between the words she'd written as if he could make it different with his brain alone. "Convenient when no one here knows the system and can check your work. Besides, it doesn't look good. The spaces you leave to fill in later are not always big or small enough for what you need to add."

"It's acceptable by all the guilds because it conveys all the necessary information and takes half the time, which means they can do with fewer scribes. You can read it for yourself, and if you find any fault with the content, I will rewrite everything."

The girl was too cheeky for her own good, but he liked that she had spunk and didn't cower before him. That didn't mean that she didn't fear him, though. He still saw it in her eyes, which made her irreverence all the more courageous or perhaps foolish.

"Far from it," he'd said. "I employ a scribe so I won't have to remember every word said in my court, and I can't tell whether everything is in there or not. Therefore, I insist on being taught this notation method so that I can make sure you record everything reliably."

Her smile had gone tight, but to her credit, Charlotte hadn't balked. "I hope you're a fast learner then, your Majesty," she'd said with a bow.

And that was how the time he should have spent catching up on his sleep ended with him spending several hours with Charlotte Cantref, his infuriating new scribe.

It had been a futile exercise to try to learn overnight a notation style that had taken her years to learn, but having her struggle to teach him without showing her frustration had been fun.

Just how petty are you prepared to be?

Bruce yawned, wind sweeping through his long, dragonish teeth as he climbed higher still. Not so petty that he ended up this fatigued regularly, that was certain. Especially not when his border checks were suddenly far more involved than they had been for years.

After the muddle in Hariston, heavy rains in the

country of Fermar had caused landslides, diverting a river and creating a physical change in its border with Trieste. The river had also flooded two towns. Bruce had been involved in the rescue efforts for a full day, flying everything from people to livestock out of the affected area to safety.

He hadn't carried people in his claws or on his back since the war, and he'd nearly forgotten what it felt like to fly with another person.

It was surprisingly enjoyable, for him at least.

The children he'd saved had been particularly enamored of the experience even if their parents had been stiff with fear. He had earned many thanks for his efforts, but none of his people could look him in the eyes as they delivered those thanks.

He was still too frightening. They still feared him, forty years later, even though he hadn't eaten or charbroiled anyone since the war.

21

KING BRUCE

*B*ruce sometimes wondered if it wouldn't be better to step down as king, put one of his cousins on the throne, and resign himself to a life centered more around his dragon self than his human form. He could build a little cottage somewhere, live a quiet life in the evenings, and act as the faithful protector during the day.

Some days that sort of freedom appealed to him.

Especially if it meant getting a break every now and then, rather than running at full speed from one disaster to another.

If the floods hadn't been enough, an outbreak of disease in a small northern town required his immediate assistance. A satchel of medicines provided to him by the healers' guild was hanging from a rope around his neck, but he didn't know if it would be enough to stop the illness in its tracks or if he would have to return again the next day with another load.

Ah, well. It was just another day in the life of the Dragon King.

Bruce was glad and grateful for the ability to help when no one else could, but perhaps he should be spending less time with his fetching scribe and getting more regenerative sleep, so his dragon self could keep providing the people invaluable assistance without dropping from the sky on them when his strength gave out.

He ought to be getting close to the afflicted town now, and there would be plenty of time to wonder about the rest of it all later.

With a slight change in the angle of his wings, he shifted his trajectory downward. After the heat of the sun beating against his black scales throughout the morning, cutting through the clouds felt like a cool shower, and by the time Bruce set down just outside of town, he felt quite refreshed.

Judging from how the town's mayor looked as she leaned against a hastily erected warning sign by the road leading into it, she wasn't feeling as well as he did.

"Your Majesty," she said, attempting a bow and almost toppling over.

"Enough, there is no need," Bruce replied, forestalling his desire to reach out and help her. Grabbing people with his clawed hands, although very dexterous and controlled, usually led to screams of fear. "I've brought medicines for you and the other townspeople."

The woman smiled at that. She was probably in her sixties, her face creased from years of work and laughter, and her hair a luminous whitish-blonde. "You have our gratitude, sire. Our local healer told us what was required to treat this sickness, but these herbs have been scarce lately."

Bruce paused in the middle of removing the package from his neck. "So I've heard, but...." He racked his brain for the memory. There was something on the edge of his recall that seemed very important. "Willowroot is one of the ingredients needed for this cure. From what I remember, this region of Trieste grows more willowroot than any other region."

The woman accepted the bundle with a sigh. "That was indeed true for many years, your Majesty. However, several seasons ago, our local willowroot crop was stricken with a blight that all but destroyed it. It is recovering slowly, but to harvest it now would mean it might never recover. The same with fireweed and hollyhock."

Oh, indeed?

Coupled with the reports that Bruce had been reading over the past week—in great detail thanks to Charlotte's tutelage—a dark suspicion formed in his mind.

It couldn't be.

Surely she wouldn't…

No, surely she would.

A growl rose in the back of Bruce's throat, but he refused to let it out. He wouldn't scare the poor woman who had come to receive his aid. "I will see what can be done to improve your harvests," he managed after a moment. "Perhaps transplant some southern varieties up here and see if they can take root. It would at least give you more resources while you wait for your own plants to recover."

The mayor smiled and clutched the medicine to her chest. "You are as wise as you are kind, sire." She inclined her head and left before Bruce could manage to find the proper words to repay the unexpected compliment.

KING BRUCE

*B*ruce waited until the mayor was gone, and all was silent again before flaring his wings menacingly. "Come forth, witch," he snarled. "Come and face me."

A delighted laugh split the air, tinkling like a silver bell, and a moment later, a woman stepped out of the shadows of the trees—a very familiar, very unwelcome woman. Her dark hair hung down past her back, shining and lustrous, and her buxom figure was accentuated by the tight corset she wore. Her face was beautiful, but the avarice in her eyes as she regarded him peeled away the illusion of physical beauty to show the ugliness inside.

"Rozia!" Bruce snarled.

"Well done!" she applauded sarcastically. "I thought it would take another disaster or two for you to figure out what was happening."

Bruce took a slow step toward her, fire building in the pit of his stomach. "I should burn you to a crisp, witch."

"Mind your temper with me," Rozia snapped. "You can't kill me, not as a dragon or as a man. And even if you could, would you risk destroying the only chance of escaping your curse?"

The witch might be lying about his inability to kill her, but she also might not. Rozia was powerful enough to turn him into a dragon and keep him from dying. She was also immortal and could cause floods and sickness or at least make them worse. The truth was that he didn't know the extent of her powers.

Still, threatening her felt good.

"I'll never be free of your curse, so I might as well do away with you and save myself the trouble of putting you on trial for treason and hanging you."

She laughed. "You think that my guild would let you put me on trial? Let me assure you, Bruce, that my actions are fully sanctioned by the guild of witches. We witches have been content to live on the sidelines of political power for too long. Seeking it has never been our way, but many of us are no longer satisfied with tying our magic to the earth alone." The darkness in her eyes deepened. "Why not also tie it to the throne? Witches could marry monarchs and produce powerful offspring with royal blood and the gift of magic. They would be unstoppable."

"That's nonsense, Rozia. Witchcraft derives its

power from the witches' connection to nature." Bruce was sure of that much, at least. "Without that connection, you don't have power."

"What is a king if not a connection to an entire nation?" Rozia asked. "You are much beloved among your people, and their love for you is a powerful force. That power can be tapped into just like the power of nature."

"Well." At least she hadn't left him in suspense. "What a shame for you that you'll never be able to verify it one way or the other because you will never become my queen."

Rozia's expression melted from greedy to something softer and more coercive. "Come now, Bruce darling," she purred, sidling up closer to him. "Don't you want what's best for Trieste? With my power tied to your position, we could do great things for our people." She ran one hand boldly down his closest claw. "No more floods…no more sickness…"

"We wouldn't have to worry about those things if you hadn't been causing them or making them worse," Bruce pointed out.

"Trifles, darling, trifles! You would never need to worry about it if you made me your queen." She came closer, scent filling his nose. Wild roses, sharp and sweet…

And yet Bruce inexplicably found himself longing for the scents of ink and paper.

"Marry me, Bruce," Rozia murmured. "Accept my

hand, and you will never need to fear for the state of Trieste again. I will give you powerful and beautiful children, I will give you love and safety, I will give you anything you can dream of. Perhaps you would like to also be the king of Glorian? Of Fermar? There is no limit to what we might do together, my darling."

Bruce jerked away from her encroaching hand. "You promise war and peace in the same breath while wearing a smile on your face," he said bitterly. "Nothing that comes out of your mouth can be believed."

"I—"

"No." He shook his massive head. "I will never marry you."

"Then I will never stop." Rozia's expression shifted from seductive to severe in the blink of a dragon's eye. "Until you marry me, your kingdom will be plagued by one disaster after another." She took a step back and put her hands on her hips. "How long will you make your people suffer out of foolish pride, hmm?" Her eyes narrowed. "The only one standing in the way of our glorious future together is you. I have waited for you for forty years but will not wait any longer. You will make me the queen of Trieste and the mother of your children, or your life shall forever be split between day and night, dragon and man. And if you think what I've pulled so far was bad," Rozia smiled sharply, "you have no idea of what's coming next."

Bruce couldn't stop himself from reaching out with

his clawed hand to grab Rozia and squeeze the life out of her, but she vanished before he could touch her, and only the echo of her laughter was left lingering in the air around him.

That and the smell of roses, which was now forever spoiled for him.

The wicked witch hadn't lied about his inability to kill her. She was too powerful, and other than accepting her demands, there was nothing he could do to stop her from wreaking havoc on his kingdom.

CHARLOTTE

*I*t didn't take a genius to figure out that something was wrong with King Bruce.

Not that Charlotte was paying that close attention to him. Since her initial kerfuffle a week ago, when she'd gotten herself locked out of the palace and stuck in the courtyard garden during sundown, she'd been careful to keep herself far away from his landing spot.

She wouldn't be responsible for another incident, no thank you. They would continue as king and scribe, and everything would keep going just fine. Bruce was broody, and he didn't smile much, but he was no longer as intimidating as he had been that first day, and she enjoyed spending time with him, especially during the night when it was just the two of them.

She didn't want to toot her own horn, but he seemed much calmer, and she couldn't help but think it was her doing. Despite his gruffness and comments that bordered on rudeness, he seemed to enjoy spending time with her.

But tonight, something was wrong. Really wrong.

Despite being halfway across the castle, Charlotte had heard his landing. A full-fledged thump indicated he'd come down far harder than usual. He'd also landed earlier than expected—it had been at least half an hour before sunset—and he'd immediately bellowed for the doors to be locked.

Now the courtyard was filled with the sounds of ripping and shredding, and it wasn't until someone actually dared to open a window and peek outside that they realized what was happening.

"Oh, gods above," one of the servants whimpered, "not the rose bushes. They were his mother's."

"He's pulling out the rose bushes?" Charlotte exclaimed, moving in to get a look for herself.

"He's destroying them!" Two other servants exchanged concerned glances. "What could have happened to set him off like that? He loved those roses."

"Perhaps he is disgusted at having such nosy servants," a familiar and sardonic voice said from behind them.

Charlotte and the servants whirled around to face Lord Oren.

"Apologies, milord!" said one of the servants as they all dropped curtsies.

Charlotte kept her eyes up as she did and saw the trepidation on the chamberlain's face. He was just as concerned as they were by the king's actions.

"The king deserves his privacy," he went on. "Now, be off with you."

The other three women scurried away, but when Charlotte went to go with them, Lord Oren shook his head. "A moment, Miss Cantref."

"Of course."

Lord Oren seemed to be steeling himself. "I'm about to ask you to do something very unconventional and something that could get us both in trouble. I would not normally ask this of you, but I fear that the king will not appreciate the appearance of anyone he isn't comfortable with right now."

Trepidation mixed with a heap of curiosity rose up in Charlotte. "What do you want me to do?"

"The sun is nearly set," Lord Oren pointed out. "Soon he'll be human again, but since he got here so early, we didn't have time to prepare the usual things for him. No clothing to put on, no food, and no weapon to defend himself with."

Ah. "Do you want me to gather these things for you?" Charlotte asked.

"I have them already. I want you to deliver them with me and distract King Bruce while I put them under the bench."

Wait, what?

"I...I don't know that I'm the right choice to help

you with this," Charlotte said weakly. "He's known you his whole life and me for only a week!"

"And yet he opens his doors to you, spends long hours in your company, and allows you to instruct him in new ways of doing things, which he has never done before." Oren's eyes were soft as he regarded her. "You've made an impression on him, Miss Cantref, a positive one. Yet I haven't seen the king in such a foul mood since the war. Perhaps something happened today to remind him of it or make him lose himself in other bad memories. Your presence will help him recall that those bad times have passed." He looked at her with worry in his blue eyes. "Will you help me?"

Charlotte was frozen momentarily, unsure whether she ought to say yes. True, the king had been less of an utter ass to her over the past days, but he hadn't done anything to make her think she was anything special. The tea he offered her in his chambers once she'd confessed that she was partial to chamomile was just a common courtesy, and the way he'd let her go early last night after she began to yawn...

Suddenly the noise from the courtyard stopped, and after a moment, Charlotte heard a low groan.

"Let's go," she said firmly.

Lord Oren gathered a bundle of things and opened the nearest door, and the two of them stepped into a place that was only vaguely recognizable as the orderly courtyard it used to be.

Every single rose bush had been ripped out of the ground and torn apart. If that wasn't enough, the grass that had filled the center of the courtyard had been gouged out so badly that it was little more than a pile of dirt against the stonework beneath it.

King Bruce was stretched out beside that pile, naked and shaking as he tried to push to his feet and failed.

Momentarily horrified by the transformation of the grounds, Charlotte let Lord Oren go ahead of her with the clothes and food. After all, she couldn't appear before her king looking as though she were horrified or disgusted with him. She wasn't, but he might misinterpret her expression of concern and fear for him.

He might not be the most courtly of men, but he was kind in his own way, and she wasn't going to repay his kindness with pain.

Taking a deep breath, she patted her cheeks to rosy them up, and once the king had at least his trousers on, she stepped forward.

"What an excellent season for a change," Charlotte said brightly, making her way around mutilated rose canes and beheaded flowers as she crossed the cobblestones. "Have you considered lilacs instead? They come in such lovely colors, you know—far more than just blue and purple and the like! You can get lilacs in pink, in yellow—I actually saw a dark red lilac on a bush in my home village. It was grown by the family that lived there, and it smelled divine." She inhaled expansively. "You haven't lived until you've visited my village during the blooming season and toured the gardens. We're known for our floriculture. It's amazing that I was able to get my parents to agree to send me to the scholars' center when they always assumed I'd go into horticulture like the rest of the family, and—"

"Enough," King Bruce said hoarsely.

Charlotte stared at him and almost blanched. He looked awful, with dark circles around his eyes and a hollowness that made it seem like he was barely hanging on to life.

Well, to hell with that.

"I agree, that's enough exercise for one day, isn't it? Here." She reached into the bundle that Lord Oren had brought along with him and pulled out a roll filled with meat and cheese. "Have a snack. It's really good cheese today, the soft kind made from—is it sheep? Or goats? Is there a difference? Can you really tell?"

"Anyone can tell," Bruce said, rolling his eyes as he took the food.

Ha, Charlotte didn't care. He could roll his eyes until they got stuck, because he had taken the food. He began to eat and devoured the roll in seconds.

She handed him another.

"Not me," she confessed, trying not to look at the exposed expanse of his muscular chest. "I'm quite bad at telling one type of cheese from another. I can spot a change in a text from fifty feet away and do well enough with flowers, but I'm quite slow to learn many other things. If you come with me to the dining hall, you can point out some of the finer aspects of telling cheeses apart."

She shouldn't have patted her cheeks to make them rosy because they were probably flaming red right now.

Once the king no longer looked like death and her worry had subsided, she couldn't ignore that he was half naked and looking far better than any king had a right to look.

"It's called having a sense of taste." Fortunately for her, Bruce pulled on the shirt Oren handed him.

"Come." He offered her his arm and pretended to let her lead him away from the ruins of the courtyard.

Lord Oren rushed ahead of them, clearing the way so no one intercepted them on the way to the dining hall.

He was damn good at not only his job but also being a true friend to the king.

Now Charlotte would have to see if she could manage the same.

KING BRUCE

*T*wo hours later, Bruce was still flummoxed about what was happening. Somehow his day had gone from utterly abysmal to the worst he'd had in years and then to one of the best he could remember simply by spending time with Charlotte.

What was it about her that made being in her presence so easy?

Perhaps it was her newness and the fact that she didn't have a history in the castle or even in the city, and therefore didn't have many expectations for him to meet. Or perhaps it was that despite her sweet exterior, she had a spine made of iron.

Or perhaps there was just something about her that he found relaxing.

Whatever it was, Bruce was grateful for it.

He ought to be hearing petitions instead of enjoying his scribe's company, but Charlotte and Oren had persuaded him to take the evening off, assuring him that no one was waiting for him that couldn't wait for the next day or even longer.

Admittedly, sitting in his quarters with a vast feast spread across the table and Charlotte on the side of it was a much more pleasant way to spend the evening. After the week he'd had, Bruce figured that he deserved it.

She'd gone from "let's eat in the dining hall" to "let's organize a private banquet" fairly quickly. The extra food was a welcome distraction after his long flight and the shameful display in the courtyard.

So was watching her nibble at some of it.

"They jelly it?" she demanded, jiggling one of the little pots with a look of disgust on her face.

"They do."

"But why? What sort of person looked at this in its original state and thought, 'Oh my, how delightfully rank. Do you know what would be even better? If we made it see-through and wobbly!'"

Bruce laughed. "Well, you're not going to sell many people on the idea of it like that."

"I wasn't trying to," Charlotte said with a sniff. "But I'll have you know that I'm quite persuasive when I want to be. If whoever makes this needs help finding people to sell it to, I have no doubt that I'll do a fantastic job of it."

"I daresay you would." She had a way about her when it came to getting people invested, Bruce concluded. "Shall we move straight on to dessert, then?"

"Gods above, yes." She looked avidly at the platter of sweets they'd somehow managed not to ravage up until now. "Is that cinnamon? I adore cinnamon."

"It is. Go on, try it." He watched her lift the pastry to her mouth, took in her moan of approval and the way she wet her lips with her tongue afterward, catching any errant crumbs...and found himself starting to get hard.

Damn it.

At least there was a table between them.

He ought to settle in a few moments.

He did not.

Now that the thought was in his head, he couldn't get it out.

Charlotte... was the first woman he'd been genuinely attracted to in a long time. There had never been any point before; why bother forming an attachment to someone he could only be with at night, who would never be able to be queen without attracting Rozia's wrath?

He should do his best to kill this inappropriate attraction to his scribe here and now. Perhaps sending her away and isolating himself would do the trick, or perhaps he should fire her altogether. He could compensate her with a year's worth of salary, but Charlotte was a proud woman, and she would see it as punishment.

He couldn't do that to her.

Despite all his flaws, she seemed to see something worthwhile in him, something beyond his station and the things he could do for Trieste. She saw the man in him and seemed to like him despite all the reasons not to.

It would be a poor repayment of her kindness to send her away, and honestly...

Honestly, he didn't want to do it for his own sake, either.

She'd taken a miserable day and turned it into something he didn't want to hide away from. If only she could work the same miracle on the rest of his life, but it didn't matter either way. He wasn't going to make her go. He would have to endure it and keep his attraction to himself.

"Well, this is amazing," she declared after finishing the pastry. "And I'm very annoyed at you now, sire."

"What did I do?" Bruce asked with a smile.

"You gave me something delicious I have never seen in the staff dining room. Now I'm going to pine for it without a guarantee that I'll ever have it again."

"It's not so rare as that," he promised. "The cooks know I prefer it, so they keep some made for me. I'll tell them to have one delivered to your room every morning if you like it."

Charlotte's eyes widened. "You would do that for me? Really?"

Uh-oh. Had he already gone too far? It was too late

not to support his own idea, though. Indecisiveness was not a good trait for a king. "Yes. I just said so."

A smile bloomed across her lovely face. "How kind! Perhaps not every day. Otherwise, my fingers will get too plump to hold my pens, but every now and then as a treat would be perfect."

"I'll see to it," Bruce promised.

"Thank you, sire. Um." Charlotte looked away momentarily, her hands fiddling with the light blue napkin the cooks had provided with the meal. "I don't mean to upset you by asking, but…"

Oh. Of course, she wanted to know why he'd been in such a rage earlier. Had he frightened her? If it had been Oren asking, Bruce might not have answered, but since it was Charlotte, well… She seemed to be the exception to a great number of his rules.

"Go ahead and ask."

"Oh, well, just…do you know how to play that lute in the corner?"

Bruce blinked. That wasn't what he'd been expecting at all. "Excuse me?" he stammered.

"The lute." She pointed to the far corner of his room where, sure enough, his lute had been sitting and collecting dust for decades now. "I was just wondering because it looks like a personal instrument, given the scenes painted on it, and if there was one thing I wish we got more of at the scholars' center, it was music. They were big on learning, but there's another institute for performance and bards and the like, which I rarely visited. I love listening to music so much, but...." Charlotte was blushing bright red now. "I'm sorry, this is so terribly inappropriate of me. I'll just go and—"

No, don't go!

"The lute is mine," Bruce interjected before she could actually talk herself into leaving. "My mother was also a lover of music. She's the one who taught me to play. I haven't picked it up in years, but..." But he would do so for her. "I would play for you, but first, I need to get the strings changed and the instrument tuned. Otherwise, I fear I might injure your ears with the sounds I'd produce."

"Ha!" Charlotte laughed a bit too loudly, clearly relieved. "I'm tougher than you think. If that noise you made earlier couldn't break me, a little lute playing certainly won't."

Bruce went still, shame surging through him, and a moment later, Charlotte seemed to realize what she'd just said.

"Oh." She clapped her hands over her mouth. "I'm so sorry, my lord! I always do this. I end up putting my foot in it even when I know better. I really ought to go this time."

He wouldn't stop her if she wanted to. But... "If you wish, I'll explain why I was so angry when I returned," he offered.

The room was utterly silent for a long moment. Charlotte seemed to be weighing something in her mind, an internal debate that Bruce couldn't follow and didn't want to. If she wanted to go, he would let her. If she stayed, then…well.

"Tell me, please," she said.

A wave of gratitude that he hadn't been expecting rolled through him. "If you're sure."

"I am. Please."

Bruce paused to wet his throat and strengthen his resolve with a gulp of wine from his goblet, then sat back and told her what had happened in the tiny town to the north, and of the confrontation between him and Rozia.

It felt good to let it all out for once, and by the time he was done talking, he felt as light as a feather.

CHARLOTTE

*C*harlotte was so furious on Bruce's behalf that she could barely breathe.

That evil bitch! To think she would not only use a desperate bargain to keep Bruce a dragon until he gave in to her, but that she would go beyond the bounds of their original agreement in an attempt to force his hand!

The greed, the entitlement, the, the...cupidity!

"You must think me a fool."

The words took a moment to break through the haze of Charlotte's anger, but when she looked at Bruce and saw the resignation in his face, she quickly let go of her rage. He wasn't the hateful one, after all. "No, of course not! You made a deal for the welfare of your country and your people that saved thousands of lives. How could I find that foolish?"

"I made that deal with a witch," he pointed out.

"So what?" she demanded. "People make deals with witches all the time. And the honorable ones, the ones who aren't out there to benefit themselves before everyone else, abide by not only the letter but by the spirit of those deals. In this case, she isn't really even abiding by the letter! She's actively making things worse for you in an attempt to force you into giving her what she wants, which undermines your free will. No legal scholar would ever try to write a defense of that kind of behavior. We have so many laws against it."

Bruce smiled slightly. "How do you know what a legal scholar would think of the case?"

Charlotte snorted indelicately. "As a scribe, I had to learn the jargon for over a dozen specialized professions. The law was one of those. What good would I be if I didn't even know how to spell the words I was asked to write down?"

Law had been one of the more challenging fields for Charlotte to conquer, but she'd managed it in the end.

"Truly?" Bruce looked surprised. "I had no idea your studies required such broad knowledge of subjects. I thought it…ah…"

Oh, now he was trying to avoid offending her. That was sweet but unnecessary. Charlotte had heard it all. "You thought we just wrote down whatever people said without paying attention to what we were recording," she offered. "Little better than an automaton with enough memory to put words on a page and then forget it all. I understand. That's what many people think of scribes, but there's a reason it takes over a decade to master the skills needed to do this job well. There's so much to understand, and we work with experts in the field to ensure we handle their needs properly."

"I didn't know it took so long to become a scribe. What other sorts of jobs take special training?"

Charlotte opened her mouth to speak, then closed it briefly before saying, "You don't have to ask simply to be kind, you know. I know it's not interesting for a lot of people and I don't want to bore you. You're the king. It must be against some kind of law to bore the king!"

"You've been working in my court all week," he pointed out. "Do you think most of the cases I hear are exciting?"

Charlotte grinned. "Okay, no. Most of them are very boring, that's true. You know, I'm sure Lord Oren would be willing to go through them beforehand and make sure you only had to deal with the interesting ones in person. It would lighten your load significantly."

Bruce shook his head. "As much as I trust Oren—and I do, he's known me since we were both young men—it's not his responsibility to be the final arbiter of what's necessary for me to handle and what isn't. The details are what can make or break them. You've seen some of those cases yourself. You know what I'm talking about."

Like the one with the woman whose cousins wished to take over her family business.

"Honestly, I prefer the boring cases to the exciting ones," Bruce went on, running a hand through his messy hair. That left it standing up in places, making him look a lot younger than he'd seemed just a moment ago. "The interesting ones usually mean a lot is at stake and people are behaving badly. I don't like having to deal with those. Not to say I won't, it's my job, but I don't do so eagerly."

"I see." Charlotte watched Bruce stifle a yawn and made a decision. "Well, given that tonight's court session is canceled, it would probably be best for you to catch up on your sleep."

"Oh." He looked a bit startled as she stood up. "I— no, there's no reason for you to leave."

He wants me to stay!

The thought spread like warm honey through Charlotte's core, putting a smile too bright to conceal on her face. But...

"You haven't even had a bath yet," she pointed out. "And this is a chance for me to organize the week's cases for the archives. I'll have them to you by the time you wake up tomorrow morning."

Bruce looked pensive. "I fear that I'm working you too hard."

"Oh, not at all!" Charlotte insisted. "I like it! I'm

learning so much, and with the shorthand, it's really quite doable for me to stay on top of things for the most part. Besides…" She bit her lip, then said, "There's always tomorrow night, right?"

"If you're sure you want to come back." His eyes were still serious, even as his expression lightened a bit. "I truly don't want to take up all your free time. I know we got off to a rocky start, but I would never try to stake a claim on more than you're willing to give."

The man is the king. The king! And he's more protective of my time than any of my instructors ever were. Or any of my gentleman friends, for that matter.

Charlotte smiled. "You're not asking me for anything that I'm not glad to give. I want to spend time with you." She took a deep breath, then said daringly, "In fact, I'm glad to spend as much time with you as you'll let me have."

Bruce's lips slowly turned up in a matching smile. "That could be all evening and all night, every evening and night if you're not careful."

"Sounds just about right." Well, now that her cheeks were undoubtedly flame-red, it was time to wrap this up. "I'd better go and finish my work, but I'll see you again tomorrow. Perhaps we can spend some time planning what you want to change about the courtyard." She didn't give him time to feel guilty again. "You really ought to add some seating for the petitioners. It has to be fatiguing to stand there for hours waiting to be let in and not daring to sit down on the cobblestones because they are afraid of looking slovenly, you know? And—" *And stop now*! "And we'll talk more tomorrow."

"Yes," Bruce said, looking a little dazed. "Tomorrow. That sounds excellent."

"Lovely." Before she could stop herself, she blew Bruce an air kiss, then turned and walked briskly to the door.

She glanced back only once as she closed it behind her, catching him staring at her, one hand outstretched like he wanted to reel her back in.

The king liked her. He really did.

No, not the king. Bruce liked her.

Charlotte closed the door with a sense of grateful satisfaction, then headed not to her room, where the paperwork she'd already completed was located, but to the castle library.

It was time to see what she could find on the topic of witches.

KING BRUCE

*A*fter forty years of what was essentially solitude, living a life of service that bore little resemblance to the future he could have had, Bruce was astonished to find himself...well, the only word for it was "courting."

Charlotte wasn't the sort of woman he would have pursued in his youth, as his parents would have insisted on a noble, but that wasn't a bad thing.

Few people, much less noblewomen, were as interesting as Charlotte Cantref.

For starters, she was fearless. Absolutely fearless. Not in a way that made Bruce wonder if she would do something foolish, but in that she threw herself into the things that interested her without hesitation or reserve. When he asked for her help redesigning the courtyard, he ended up with three complete sets of plans, each with a slightly different focus.

"This one prioritizes space for petitioners," she said as she laid the drawing out before him—yet another talent of hers that he hadn't known about. "This one brings more of the natural world into the castle, and it will save space for a few trees by the doors here." She pointed at the spot. "And this one offers the most space for you as you land in the evenings. I also think you should have a small pavilion or a gazebo where you can dress privately, eat at a table, and lie down to rest before entering the castle. You know, for the times that you are a bit more fatigued than usual. It's important to think about your comfort."

It was?

Bruce couldn't remember the last time anyone had prioritized his comfort so openly. His servants were excellent and dutiful, of course, and he was never wanting for comfort when he was inside the castle. But Charlotte was thinking about both the man and the dragon. She was considering every side of him and sharing her ideas about what he might like best.

It was only fair that he return the favor. "What about something that blends a little bit of everything?" he asked, pointing to different aspects he appreciated. "Stackable seating that can be moved—simple benches would be easy to store along the walls back here. Three should be sufficient. That takes up the room for the trees, but we can keep the lilac bushes in place of the roses without sacrificing space for me to land. Usually, I have plenty of space—you could fit two of me in here, and I wouldn't normally have a problem. What do you think?"

He looked up and was surprised to find Charlotte staring at him with a slightly dazzled expression. "What's wrong?" he asked.

"You really want the lilac bushes?"

"Well, you like them so much. Why shouldn't they have a place in the castle? I won't add any rose bushes again, so…" He had nightmares with that scent pervading his nose and had woken up swinging once because he thought Rozia was right there. "But you'll have to pick them out," he added. "I'm not very good at choosing the right combination of colors. Of course, I'll provide you with the funds to make the purchases."

"Of course." Her smile was wide and a trifle watery. "I'd be delighted to! I know the best kinds, trust me, they'll grow and grow and have this whole castle smelling like bliss for months on end."

"That sounds good."

It sounded incredible, but he didn't want to gush like a maiden.

"It will be," she promised him. "What do you think about the prospect of—"

As the door suddenly banged open, Bruce stood up incensed, determined to tear a stripe off whoever had entered his room so rudely—but it was Lord Oren, and he looked frantic.

"Sire! Come quickly, the stables are ablaze!"

The stables? Oh, gods above…

"Have the horses been saved?" he asked, moving immediately toward the door.

"I think so, the hands have seen to that, but the wind is kicking up. Right now, we have just one structure burning, but if we don't move fast…"

Oh, hells. Not the castle, which was made of stone, but so much of Ashelvin was old, dry wood. "It could set the city ablaze. Wake everyone up," he snapped.

It was a little after midnight, and most castle servants were likely asleep. "We need to arrange carry lines from the wells to the stable. Pull assistance from the nearest quarters, and—" He stalled as Charlotte stepped up beside him. "What are you doing?"

"Coming with you, of course!" she exclaimed. "You said everyone is needed for carrying water!"

"Yes, but—" *But not you, not the woman I'm falling increasingly in love with every day. I couldn't bear it if something bad happened to you.*

Charlotte's eyes narrowed. "Whatever you're about to say, don't," she said and ran out in front of him toward the stables.

Bruce gritted his teeth and followed her, running out into a scene of chaos and red-tinged, smoky light.

The stables were behind the castle, which would help a bit when it came to protecting the rest of the city. A sudden gust of wind lifted Charlotte's hair, almost sending it back into Bruce's face. They needed to make progress fast, or the sparks would fly and set other buildings alight.

There was already a ragged chain of people running back and forth from one of the wells in the least efficient way possible. Bruce stepped in, grateful his voice carried so far even when he wasn't in his dragon form. "Stop running with that bucket! You're slopping half of it out on the ground before it even gets to the fire!" he shouted. Gradually, the people stopped moving and started listening.

"Line up! Adults pass the buckets, and children act as runners for the empties. You, you, and you—go wake the people near the east wall and get a crew like this going from the well over there." Bruce heard a distant whickering sound and was grateful when he saw a horse running toward them, unbridled but unburned. "You and you!" He pointed at two of the stable hands. "Round up the horses and lead them into the castle courtyard. Make sure they have water and people they know around them to help them stay calm."

"Now get moving!"

People started flowing into action far more smoothly than they had a minute ago.

Charlotte gamely joined the line of bucket passers while Bruce got closer to the fire to assess the damage and see what could be done.

The answer was—nothing.

Whatever had started this fire must have flared up hot and fast, too fast for the hands who spent the night in the stables to realize until it was too late.

Whoever started this fire?

You know who's responsible for this.

A fire like this didn't blast out of nowhere. Bruce had expected Rozia to strike again. He just hadn't expected her to strike so close to home.

CHARLOTTE

*C*harlotte leaned against the castle's outer wall, too tired to hold herself up even one moment longer. She stank of sweat and smoke, her dress was singed right through in a few places, and her arms and back ached from passing bucket after bucket full of cold, heavy water. She coughed into her fist, her throat hoarse from a combination of shouting and breathing in foul air for hours.

Despite everyone's best efforts, the fire had spread to two nearby buildings. Both had been evacuated, and thanks to their slate roofs they hadn't immediately gone up, but it seemed like as soon as one little fire was put out, another erupted somewhere else.

The sky was full of cinders, and standing amongst it all had felt uncomfortable, like being a part of the darker myths in their people's distant past.

It wasn't until dawn that the fiery frenzy had finally ended, and only because Bruce was able at last to transform into his dragon self, spread his immense wings, and bring a gust of wind down that prostrated everyone within a hundred feet of it as it smothered every last flame, saving the two buildings from becoming infernos.

The stables were a total loss, but at least the horses and grooms had survived.

It could have been so much worse, so why was Charlotte so...so angry?

Was it because she was tired?

Because she felt so heartsick?

Or was it the glimpses she kept catching of a woman in a purple dress who had watched the scene with open glee?

There was no way for Charlotte to verify that the woman she'd spotted was Rozia, but she knew for sure that it hadn't been a hallucination.

She'd seen her three times in different spots around the burning stables.

Charlotte would have told Bruce, but he was busy and had given her this task, which she would fulfill to the best of her ability.

She wasn't about to let him down. He was her king, after all.

More than just your king.

You should admit it, at least to yourself.

You love him.

Yeah, she did, but she wouldn't tell him that soon. Or ever.

Immediately after the fire was out, Bruce had taken off, likely to survey the city and see if trouble was brewing anywhere else, and with him gone Lord Oren had taken charge of organizing everything.

Good, he was welcome to it.

Charlotte could just fall asleep right where she was, leaning against the wall.

"Miss Cantref." A warm voice and a soft hand on her shoulder jolted her out of her brief doze, reminding her of just how damn uncomfortable it was to fall asleep standing up. "Get inside," Lord Oren said as soon as her eyes focused on him. "Get cleaned up and head to bed. No court will be held tonight, so you can rest properly and not worry about catching up on your paperwork."

"But...shouldn't I..." There had to be more she could do, some other way she could be helping Bruce right now.

"All you should do is take care of yourself. I'll handle everything else." He smiled at her. "Good work." He patted her shoulder and then left.

Charlotte struggled to muster the willpower to move.

The thought of a cool bath—not hot, she might never want to be hot again—provided the motivation she needed. She groaned, pushed off the wall, and staggered toward the nearest door.

She was one of the last to enter.

Apparently, most of the people who had worked relentlessly throughout the night were more sensible than she and had headed to bed once the emergency was over.

Mmm, bed...a comfortable, warm bed where she would feel safe and relaxed...

Charlotte wasn't even cognizant enough to realize that she'd turned down Bruce's private hallway and headed straight into his room instead of her own. She forgot about getting clean, she forgot her ravenous hunger, she forgot everything in the soft embrace of that bed. All she knew was that she was exhausted, and this place smelled wonderful, and the bed was so soft it felt like falling onto a cloud.

All Charlotte knew was pure comfort, and after the terrible night she'd had, that was enough to let her fall into a deep, dead-to-the-world sleep.

She only stirred twice—once when a gasp of recognition echoed in the room and again when a thick, warm blanket was draped over her with no care for how dirty it might get against her clothes.

The third time Charlotte woke up was due to a dry mouth and a painfully full bladder. She flopped an arm out from under the covers, reaching for the glass of water she kept on the little table beside her bed.

Gods, she could drain a pitcher right now. She...wait.

Where was the water?

Where was the table?

Where was she?

"Ah, you're finally awake." A warm, familiar voice drew her attention toward the foot of the bed. She twisted her aching neck, not quite believing what she was seeing, but—nope, not a dream. There was Bruce, sitting in a chair with a lap full of paperwork, looking tired but pleased somehow. The wall behind him was covered by a familiar tapestry, and there were the double doors to the balcony that he flew out of each morning, and…and…

Oh shit. Charlotte had put herself to bed in Bruce's room.

"I was beginning to wonder if I needed to call for a healer," Bruce said, politely ignoring her freak-out. "You've been sleeping for a long time but must have needed it."

"How long?" Charlotte asked meekly.

"Since a bit after sunrise this morning, I understand, until now…about fourteen hours."

She was the worst! Fourteen hours! Had she been taking over his bed and invading his privacy for fourteen hours?

"I'm so sorry," Charlotte said, trying to hide her misery and clearly not succeeding very well if the startled look he threw her was any indicator. "I didn't mean to come here and inconvenience you, I promise. I would never invite myself into your space in such a way if I wasn't completely out of my head, I—"

"Charlotte." Bruce's quiet but insistent voice broke through her babbling. "I'm not offended by anything you've done."

"But I—"

"I liked finding you here when I came back." Now his face was turning red, a match to hers. "Perhaps... we can continue this conversation after you've had a chance to clean up from this morning."

"Yes, I—oh, your bed!" It was filthy now, residue from her clothes and skin turning the sheet beneath her from white to grey.

"I don't care about the bed," Bruce said firmly. "Go and get cleaned up, then come back here for dinner. We can talk then."

He wanted to talk? About what? Maybe he'd detected her affection for him and decided now was the time to let her down easy.

"All right," Charlotte said with a deep sigh, getting up from the bed and heading for the door.

Once out in the hallway, she sighed even more deeply, then grimaced.

Necessities first, melancholy later. She really needed to use the privy.

KING BRUCE

*B*ruce wasn't the type to be given to self-doubt. He was who he was, and after so many years of being him, he wasn't about to change. With everything he had to worry about, there was no room in his life for that.

Except...

He was changing because of Charlotte. She hadn't even been here a month, and she'd already changed something fundamental about the way he looked at the world. Time was for more than just fulfilling his duties and keeping his people safe and fed; hope was for more than just caring for everyone else.

With Charlotte, Bruce was looking forward to more than just being a source of help and comfort for Trieste's people. He wondered if possibly, just maybe, she was someone he could comfort more...directly.

And be comforted by in turn.

Although, from the look on her face as she'd darted out of his suite, he might be way off in his appraisal of her feelings for him.

Charlotte had not realized where she was going when she'd headed to his rooms instead of her own, and when he had woken her up, she'd been mortified to find herself in his bed.

"She didn't mean to come here," he rationalized aloud as he stripped the bed himself. He didn't want any servants to be around when she returned.

He needed privacy to talk things out with Charlotte.

"She was so tired she didn't even know where she was going this morning. She might have ended up anywhere...."

But she hadn't.

Charlotte had ended up in his bed.

When he'd found her there after finally stomping into his rooms, more than a little disappointed that he hadn't gotten to meet her in the courtyard right after his transformation, his upset had turned into joy.

She hadn't come to meet him because she was already waiting for him to return to her in his room. She'd been snoring gently, soft little whirrs muffled against the down of his pillow, and he hadn't been able to resist covering her up.

As one hour of sleep stretched into another, Bruce had directed Oren to bring him everything related to the fire so that he could get a little work done without leaving Charlotte.

Oren had taken one look inside and smiled, then promised he'd leave someone posted nearby so food could be brought immediately when Charlotte woke up.

Speaking of…

At the sound of a quick knock, Bruce walked to the door and pulled it open to reveal one of the cooks' assistants holding a tray laden with a dozen different foods over his head.

"Evening, sire," the lad said with a smile that was bordering on a grimace. "Where should I put this down?"

"Right here." Bruce showed him to the table and helped him set the massive tray down, then nodded in response to the low bow the young man gave him. "I'll leave it outside the room for you to pick up later," he said.

"Aye, sire. Um." The lad fidgeted with the hem of his tunic for a moment. "May I speak, your Majesty?"

Bruce nodded.

"Then please, sire, allow me to give you my most humble thanks for the aid you gave us all during the fire," the lad blurted. "My whole family lives in one of the houses what nearly went up, and my grandmam can't get out of bed anymore. Could have been very bad for us if you hadn't been there to save them all."

Oh, if he only knew that Bruce was the reason the fire had been set in the first place.

He wasn't positive because he hadn't seen Rozia himself, but even through the smoke and ash, he'd detected the cloying whisper of her rose-scented perfume.

"I did what I had to," Bruce said. "It's my duty to protect my people, and there's no need to thank me for doing my job."

"Maybe not," the young man allowed with a little smile. "But I want to do it anyway, sire. Begging your pardon." After receiving Bruce's nod, he bowed again and let himself out the door. "Evening, Miss Cantref," Bruce heard him say as he left, and—

Oh.

There she was.

Charlotte stepped inside, clean once more, her slightly wet, golden hair pulled back in a braid and her usual scribe's dress set aside for a simpler, pale pink smock tonight. With her hands clasped in front of her and an expression of determination on her lovely face, she looked like everything Bruce had never known he'd wanted until now.

He opened his mouth to say as much, but the words remained stuck in his throat for some reason.

What if she didn't feel the same way?

What if she was about to tell him that she couldn't stay here any longer, that she was uncomfortable with the way he'd drawn her in close, so close she couldn't tell her private rooms from his in her fatigue?

What if she was about to—

"Oh, for goodness' sake," Charlotte muttered. She marched across the room, wrapped her arms around Bruce's shoulders, leaned in, and kissed him soundly on the mouth.

She was slightly off-center, their noses squishing before he tilted his head to accommodate them, and the pressure was so hard that his teeth pressed uncomfortably against his lips before Charlotte eased off a bit.

It was the most delightful kiss he'd ever experienced, even counting the misty days of his youth when he'd been more than happy to trade kisses with a fair maid in a dark corner of the castle.

The past forty years had been barren of physical affection...until now.

Until Charlotte.

Bruce's heart opened, and every sweet and tender thing he'd refused to let himself experience for decades flooded in all at once. He reached out and slid his arms around her waist, pulling her closer as the kiss deepened.

She made a humming sound of satisfaction and finally pulled back to let out a gasp. "I'm so happy that I was right! Otherwise, this would have been really awkward."

"What, grabbing your king and having your wicked

way with him?" Bruce asked, a little surprised he was comfortable enough to joke with her but happy when she laughed.

"Yes! When I left your room earlier, I...well, let's just say that I didn't think this would be the reception I got when I returned." She sighed and leaned into him a bit harder. "I worried that I'd overstepped the mark. I worried it was just me and that I was making you uncomfortable. Then I saw how you looked at me, and I thought...well, no man would look at a woman like that if he didn't feel anything for her. Right?"

"Right." Bruce probably would have agreed to anything she said right now.

He was still reeling that his love was requited, despite all the difficulties that were bound to come up with it.

He opened his mouth to name some of them, then shut it again.

Those difficulties were real, but they could wait. Everything else could wait. Right now, all he wanted to do was to be with Charlotte, kiss her and hold her and share a meal with her, and revel that she wanted to do the same things with him.

The real world would intrude soon enough, but until then, Bruce would take whatever he could of this incredible new experience.

29

CHARLOTTE

*W*hile in school, Charlotte had occasionally thought about what it would be like to find a sweetheart, someone to fall head over heels in love with. She'd always imagined that the kind of man she'd end up with would be like her, a studious man who practiced a trade or skill of some sort. Someone from a similar background and station with similar hopes and aspirations. They would come together easily, naturally, like two peas in a pod.

She had fancied a few of the men she'd trained with, and she'd even gone out with a couple for a drink or a meal in town, but nothing had ever blossomed into real love.

That had been fine with her since she'd always known that she would get a position somewhere else and would probably find her love interest there.

When she'd gotten assigned to the palace and had arrived at Ashelvin, she was sure that her horizon was about to expand along with her social circle. The capital was a big city, and she had been convinced she would meet someone as ambitious and forward-thinking as she was.

Charlotte had yet to figure on that man being King Bruce, the witch-cursed, shapeshifting, heart-sore ruler of the entire nation. She hadn't expected to fall so thoroughly in love with him despite—and maybe a bit because of—his blunt, straightforward nature. And she certainly had never imagined how intense it would feel to be loved by him in return—this man she had so little in common with and yet who suited her so perfectly.

Bruce was all-or-nothing.

No part of him preferred to prevaricate or put things on hold. When he fell for her, he fell hard, and no one was left uncertain about his affections. Not Charlotte, and not the rest of the staff at the castle either.

Lord Oren was the first to figure it out, of course.

He took Charlotte aside two nights after Bruce's emotional revelation and said to her, "If this connection with our king is something you want, then I'm very happy for you. If it isn't, tell me, and I will write you the strongest letter of recommendation possible while secretly escorting you out of the city."

Charlotte was touched and offended at the same

time. "Bruce wouldn't coerce me to be with him, milord! He's not that kind of man! I just, we just, it...." She shrugged helplessly. "We fell in love."

Lord Oren's worried expression eased. "I'm happy to hear that. No one deserves it more, I'm sure. Nevertheless, come to me if you have any difficulties. In the meantime, I'll add some amenities to the king's rooms that will make both of you more comfortable."

Charlotte wasn't sure what he'd been talking about until a long, velvet-covered couch appeared against one of the walls, an additional wardrobe for some of her clothes, and a copy of the key that would allow her entrance to the suite.

She asked Bruce about it, intent on ensuring she didn't overstep. All he did was look slightly perplexed and say, "Of course I want you to have it. You're always welcome here, whether I'm in or not."

In fact, no one gave Charlotte any bother over their new relationship. The closest she came to offense was one of the chambermaids asking if she could have Charlotte's room.

"Since it's just greedy to keep it now you're sleeping with the king, ain't it?" the girl asked.

She wasn't, though. Sleeping with him. Not in the most fulsome sense of the word, at least. They cuddled in bed, and she often felt his arousal pressing against her behind when they spooned or against some other part of her in different positions. Still, Bruce never taken it further than that.

It wasn't that Charlotte was a prude.

She was the daughter of a gardener and a very proficient herbalist. She knew what went into getting pregnant and how to prevent it. She was prepared to take the necessary precautions, but so far...so far it hadn't been an issue.

First, it had just been kissing. They went no farther for weeks, kissing and cuddling on the new, very comfortable couch.

Kissing had gradually become petting over the clothes, which slowly evolved to touching beneath the clothes.

Charlotte couldn't wait to do more, to become one with Bruce in every way a man and a woman could, but he was holding back for some reason, and she didn't want to push him.

After all, he was still her king and would decide when he was good and ready to take that final step.

30

CHARLOTTE

A month after their mutual declaration of love, Charlotte found herself on the couch, on her back, her dress pulled down to the waist from her shoulders. Her small, pert breasts were displayed as Bruce knelt between her legs and sucked one of her nipples into his mouth.

"Oh…" Charlotte clasped his head with both hands, unsure whether to push him away or pull him in closer.

What he was doing felt so strange but so wonderful at the same time. When his hand found her other nipple and lightly squeezed it, she wound her fingers tight into his hair and groaned.

"That feels so good," she gasped. "Ah, so good. I didn't know… I've never felt like this before." She had used her fingers on herself down below, but she had never bothered to tease her breasts like this. "Bruce, oh…"

An ache grew steadily between her legs, and Charlotte felt herself slick with desire.

"Tell me more," Bruce murmured, briefly raising his mouth off her breast. "Tell me what you feel. Tell me what you want."

"I want…"

"Tell me."

"I want your mouth on me."

"Mmm." He smiled and nuzzled her nipple. "Like this?"

Charlotte giggled. "Not exactly, although that's lovely."

"I see. Maybe like…this?" He brushed his lips down her flushed skin until they touched her belly button, then kissed it.

"That's—" Charlotte's breath hitched as his tongue delved into the tiny indentation. "That's also won-wonderful, but…um, I was thinking perhaps a little lower."

"Ah." He sat back, picked her leg up, and pressed a kiss to her ankle. "I've got it now."

"No!" Charlotte laughed even as she grabbed one of the decorative cushions on the couch and rapped Bruce's firm waist with it. "Higher! I want your mouth to…you know…."

She knew her face had gone beet red and waited

for him to move without her needing to make the destination explicit.

He pretended to not understand.

Bastard.

"I know nothing. Where do you want my mouth to go?" Bruce asked, looking adorably and deliberately confused. "Your knee, maybe? I bet you have very sensitive knees." He pushed her skirts higher, revealing more of her pale, creamy skin.

Charlotte actually had ticklish knees, so he did not need to get caught up right there. "No, I want your mouth on my...on...."

Was she really about to ask a king to kiss her there?

Part of her wanted to flinch away, to forget it entirely, but the warm and sensual light in Bruce's eyes urged her on. "My womanhood," she said at last. "I want your mouth on my sex."

She'd heard that it was exquisitely pleasurable.

Bruce grinned. "Now that's an idea I can whole-heartedly agree with." He still went slow, skimming his hands up her thighs and very slowly pulling her undergarments down and out of the way. They were drenched in the center, and Charlotte wanted to cover her face from mortification, but Bruce seemed enthralled. "You really like me doing this," he said wonderingly. "You want me."

"Yes," Charlotte forced out, "I really, really do, so if you would please, please just touch me and—ah—"

That was his finger, slipping along the sides of her folds before finally delving into the center. His touch set her on fire, and the moment his thumb rubbed across her clit, she was gone. An orgasm stronger than it had any right to be roared through her body, leaving her shuddering and breathless and Bruce looking like the embodiment of the smug, self-satisfied man.

"That was gorgeous," he told her as soon as he had her attention again. "Shall we try it with my mouth this time?"

Charlotte nodded, and by the time they were both done, she had climaxed twice more and Bruce once with the help of her hands.

They moved to the bed and dozed side by side for a while, but after a time spent in the blissful afterglow, Charlotte's mind began to work again.

This was…he was…it was indescribable.

He made her feel so treasured, and he played her body much better than he played the lute. She thought —she hoped—that she made him feel just as treasured.

From what Lord Oren had insinuated, Charlotte was the first person Bruce had gotten intimate with since he'd been cursed. She wanted to do it all again already, to do much more. Still, there were so many complications, not the least of which was the possibility of pregnancy if they went that far.

And she definitely wanted to go that far.

She could go to an apothecary or healer here in

Ashelvin, but if the opportunity to return home presented itself, she could kill two birds with one stone. Possibly three if she got a chance to talk to her village's witch while she was there.

"Bruce," she murmured.

He pulled her a little closer. "Mmm?"

"If we're going to finish the courtyard before autumn, I ought to go get the lilacs I've got in mind."

He stilled, then got up on one elbow and looked at her, expression serious. "You want to go home?"

"Just for a day," she promised him. "Not to stay. And it's only a day's travel from here, much closer than the scholars' center. One day there, one day in my village, one day coming back. Three days total that I'll be gone, no more."

"Are you sure that's all there is?"

It made Charlotte a bit sad that he felt the need to ask. She knew it was hard for him to trust that she wanted him, really wanted him, after so long alone. "I promise," she assured him. "My parents grow all the varieties of lilac that we need, and it will be nice to see them and tell them that…that I've fallen in love."

His eyes went wide.

Oh…goodness, was this the first time she'd said it?

How terribly neglectful of her.

"I do," she promised him. "I love you. And I'll be back as soon as possible."

"I could fly you," Bruce offered.

Charlotte beamed a grin at him. "I would love to go

flying with you! That would be amazing! But…" Her enthusiasm dimmed a bit when she thought about the plants. "I know that you are big and strong in your dragon form, and you could probably carry a whole crate of flowers, but the wind would be tough on the plants. I'll have to take a wagon as is. Perhaps if you fly me there, I'll return by myself."

"Fine." He leaned down and kissed her. "Go do what must be done. Leave me to pine for you."

"You won't even notice I'm gone after you drop me off," Charlotte promised him.

Bruce smiled crookedly. "Oh, I'm sure I will."

KING BRUCE

*C*arrying someone for a longer distance, someone he was invested in protecting at all costs, was different. Bruce had flown with people in his grip before. He'd rescued countless of his subjects over the years—in everything from floods to snowstorms. He'd even carried a horse or two in his day, although that seemed to scare the poor beasts so badly that they shook for hours once he set them down again.

He thought about letting Charlotte ride on his back but quickly decided that wouldn't do. She'd be too cold, and the thought of her falling off somehow...no.

He would clasp her in his own two hands and hold her close to his chest to protect her against anything that came their way. He would keep her with the utmost care and caution.

He hadn't counted on the way she'd lean out of

his grip to get a better look at the ground as it passed by beneath them. "Incredible!" Charlotte shouted over the wind. "I never imagined the world could look like this! It all seems so small from this high up!"

Bruce, who had been flying for so long now that it had lost all sense of novelty, was chuckling. "Everything is closer than you think when you fly," he rumbled. "Are we getting close to your village?"

"We are." Charlotte pointed down at the river. "The bend, there—that's where the road from my village meets the other two from our neighbors. Just beyond the copse of trees there, and you'll see Fairdale."

Fairdale came all too quickly for Bruce, who could fly like this all day with Charlotte and never get tired of it. But he began his descent when the little hamlet, probably no more than fifty or sixty houses, came into view.

It looked like any other little Triesten village, full of quaint homes with whitewashed walls and shake roofs, but the smell...the smell was absolutely divine. Even growing up surrounded by roses, Bruce had never been as inundated by the perfume of flowers as before arriving here. He'd flown over this place many times before and paid it no heed.

See what new things can still come your way?
Your life can be more than one of duty.
You can have new experiences.
You can have love.

He did have it, right here in his arms. How would he ever let her go?

How would he go on without her someday?

Bruce needed to slow his brain down before he talked himself out of leaving Charlotte here entirely. The future was unknown. All he could do was enjoy what they had now and do his best to never give her a reason to leave him.

He set Charlotte down in a field right outside Fairdale, but it was clear that everyone in town knew he was there. The edge of the village was thronged with people whispering to each other. When Bruce looked over, the men nervously bowed as the women dropped into curtsies. Only the children seemed more excited than anxious.

"It's all right!" Charlotte called out. "Our king won't bite!"

A girl of perhaps three or four years old broke ranks and ran over to them first.

She mumbled around the pair of fingers she had stuck in her mouth, "Why's he got such big teef, den?"

"Because he needs to look scary to frighten away anyone who might want to harm Trieste," Charlotte replied instantly. "Isn't that right?" She smiled up at Bruce, who...

Um.

"Right," he said in the dragon equivalent of a whisper.

The little girl still clapped her hands over her ears.

"Wow! You're loud! I bet you can yell louder than my baby brother! Mama!" She turned and shouted toward a woman holding an infant against her chest, looking mortified. "Bring Roger over so's he can have a yelling contest with the king!"

Oh, gods.

"Unfortunately, King Bruce has to go now," Charlotte interjected, barely containing her laughter. "But I'm sure you'll see him again soon! Perhaps when your baby brother is a little older and has outgrown the worst shouting."

The girl wilted. "That will be forever. He shouts all night."

"Let's go talk to your mum about it." Charlotte leaned in and, with no apparent self-consciousness, kissed Bruce right on the edge of his scaly jaw. "Thank you for bringing me here," she said. "I'll be back in Ashelvin in two days."

"I'll see you soon, then," Bruce replied.

He waited for her to get some space before he began preparing his body for takeoff. He felt aware of himself in a way he wasn't used to, aware of his ungainliness, the heavy lines of muscle, and the long, sharp claws.

He didn't want the people of Fairdale to be afraid of him, not when they meant so much to Charlotte.

If she had her way, they wouldn't be afraid. She would talk to them about him, or at the very least talk to her parents and reassure them that she hadn't gone to work for a monster.

Hadn't fallen in love with a monster.

Bruce kicked off and sailed into the sky, unable to bear their gazes anymore. He swirled upward, watching the little village gradually become smaller and smaller until he couldn't smell the lilacs any longer and couldn't pick Charlotte out from the crowd.

There. She'd been delivered, and she was safe. Now he could go about his regular duties instead of spending every moment worrying about her...

Oh, who was he kidding? He was going to be worried about her regardless!

She's safe with her people. Now to see to the rest of your people.

There was a long list of places he had to check on today, towns where poor weather, terrible accidents, and strange incursions were leading to chaos. He had a duty to them and couldn't let even Charlotte keep him from it.

CHARLOTTE

*C*harlotte's first day back in Fairdale was filled with love and laughter. Her parents were thrilled to see her, although her father scolded her for nearly giving him a stroke when he saw her flying to them in the arms "of that great beastly thing."

"Papa," Charlotte had scolded him. "That's unkind of you. King Bruce became a dragon to save us, after all."

"That's true," her father acknowledged, looking a bit shamefaced, "but that doesn't mean I want to see him up close and personal in that form, y'know? I wouldn't mind seeing the man, of course, but we're so busy here I doubt I'll ever get to Ashelvin for one of the festivals I hear he still makes an appearance at."

"Which festivals?" Charlotte asked.

"Oh, just the big ones, love," her mother put in from where she was mending the corner of Charlotte's dress because she just couldn't help herself. "One for the start of each season. The autumn harvest festival is just around the corner, and I hear in Ashelvin it goes on for a full three days. I saw one once," she added, looking up with a smile. "When I was just a girl. They made a special dais for him in the city market, and he stood up there and spoke about how proud he was of all of us and wished for us to have a joyous and bountiful season. It was quite lovely. City officials often make announcements during the festivals as well."

"Like how they plan to tax us more," her father said with a frown.

"Like the projects they'll focus on for the next quarter," her mother amended. "Which roads would be fixed, bridges mended, that sort of thing."

"Oh." Charlotte was looking forward to it.

"That's all for later, though," her father said. "What brings you to us this time around, Charlie?"

"*Papaaaa,*" she moaned, and they all chuckled. "Actually..." Charlotte told them about the new project for the courtyard, carefully omitting how the roses came to be uprooted in the first place. Her father's eyebrows rose at the thought of contributing such an essential piece to the castle's appearance. Her mother had plenty to say about the medicinal qualities of lilacs and how they could be put to good use once they were grown. Not to mention the money Charlotte had brought to pay for so many of their plants would go a long way toward ensuring her parents' comfort.

The rest of the day passed in a blur of color choices, frequent visits from friends eager to get news of Ashelvin and the king, and more food than Charlotte could possibly eat offered by her parents.

On the second day, the day she was meant to leave and head back to the capital, Charlotte left her family home early to make a discreet trip to the village's wise woman.

Donata had worked closely with her mother for years, but Charlotte knew that she could trust the woman to keep to herself that she was there for a "special" tea.

Knocking on the old woman's door, she prayed that her face wouldn't erupt in redness once she had admitted the reason for her visit.

The door opened and—

"Ah," Donata said knowingly as she opened the door a little wider. "Looking for a special tea, dear?"

"Yes," Charlotte said meekly.

"I thought as much. The village is talking about how you got a special ride from Ashelvin from our king." She ushered Charlotte into her small, dimly lit cottage and closed the door behind her. "I can certainly understand why you'd want to be safe under the circumstances. It might be awkward to have a child with a man who's only a man half the time."

"*Yeeeees*, there's that," Charlotte said, "but I have to

confess that's not the only reason I've come to you today, mistress." Not that it wouldn't have been just as embarrassing to talk to a wise woman in Ashelvin about this, given how everyone was in everyone else's business there.

Donata paused in the act of pulling a ceramic jar down from her floor-to-ceiling shelf. "Oh? What else is on your mind?" She turned more fully to face Charlotte, her expression going hard. "You're not already expecting, are you? Because that takes an entirely different course of herbs to end, and there's no way you'll make it back to Ashelvin by tonight if you do."

"No, no," Charlotte assured her. "That's not it at all. I was just wondering…how much contact you have with the witches."

Donata froze, entirely stiff for a split second. "Why do you ask, dear?" Her voice was pleasant enough, but there was a dark undertone to it that made Charlotte nervous.

"Please." Charlotte stepped forward and impulsively took one of Donata's hands in both of hers. The old woman's skin was papery and cool, but strength was hidden. "I'm not here to cause you any harm, I swear. You've nothing to fear from me whether you're a witch or not. I just want to ask you a few questions."

Donata sighed and pulled her hand away, but not before giving Charlotte a little squeeze. "I suppose there's no harm in you asking. Just don't let that overgrown serpent of a lover of yours come after me if he doesn't like the answers that I give you. Come, sit with me at the table."

There were only two chairs, and Charlotte pulled up one while she watched Donata grab a few more jars before joining her.

As the old woman measured and blended the special tea, she made a gesture at Charlotte that clearly signaled her to get on with it.

"Is it true there's no way to break a contract with a witch once it's made?"

"It is," Donata replied immediately, and Charlotte's heart sank.

The books she'd found in the library at the castle had indicated as much, but she had held a little hope in her heart nevertheless.

"The witch is merely the representative of the bond, you see. The deal your lover made with Rozia, he made with the earth itself. There is no gainsaying the mother of us all."

"You know the details of that?"

Donata laughed dryly. "All of us know the details of that. Her bad behavior has plagued us for as long as she's been alive. I've been the wise woman in this town for over a hundred years and never had anyone question me for it until poor Bruce made a deal with the wrong witch. The year he was first changed, a mob almost burned me to death."

Charlotte pressed her hands to her mouth in horror. "Oh no! How did you survive it?"

"Oh, I went into the woods for a while and made myself scarce until tempers cooled," Donata smirked. "Not to mention, as soon as everyone's general ills became more than they could bear, the wives made their husbands apologize to me. If not open arms, I was welcomed back with at least a new level of tolerance." She laid several large, blue-tinged leaves in a mortar and began to grind them down.

A spicy scent filled the air, and Charlotte sneezed.

"Here, dear." Donata handed over a handkerchief. "What else is troubling you about witches?"

"Well...have you heard about the disasters across Trieste lately?"

"I have," Donata replied evenly.

"And you don't find them at all...suspicious?"

"Oh, I'm sure they're the work of Rozia, dear. But that's not my affair." Donata shook her head firmly. "We witches are only loosely connected via the guild. We don't make a habit of interfering in each other's ways. That only leads to mayhem, believe me. I'm sure you'll find that there have been issues everywhere there's a town without a witch who claims it."

"But the things Rozia is doing are dangerous!" Charlotte protested. "They're going to get people killed or start another war!"

Donata sighed. "And that's a tragedy, but the truth is that life is always an uncertain proposition. I'm sorry, Charlotte, but if you've come to me looking for assistance in breaking Rozia's curse or taking some action against her, you've come to the wrong place. I've no interest in involving myself."

Charlotte sighed. "It was worth a try."

"Now." Donata poured her assembled herbs into an oilcloth bag, tied it off tightly, and handed it over. "Ideally, you will drink one cup before intercourse and another after. If you get carried away beforehand, you should drink two after in short succession. One teaspoon only, in boiling water, steeped for five minutes. That will be seven silvers."

Without question, Charlotte handed over the steep fee—one didn't haggle with the village wise woman. "Thank you for talking to me," she said, holding back her frustration as she got up from the table. "I—"

The ground beneath their feet suddenly shuddered, a terrible cracking sound filling the air. Charlotte stumbled to the side, hitting the wall with her hip. Donata reeled as well, but Charlotte was able to catch her before she hit the floor. A flying shard cut into Charlotte's cheek, leaving a stinging line of pain. The herbs weren't so lucky, hundreds of carefully labeled jars smashing to the floor behind them.

Just as quickly as it began, the shaking stopped.

Charlotte made sure Donata could stand on her own before running outside. People stood in the street, clutching each other and crying as they stared at the massive crack running straight down the center of Fairdale's only road. The cobblestone path, which had only been laid a few years ago, the result of massive saving and planning on the part of the town leaders, was in total disarray. Several of the houses had semi-toppled over. Thank the gods, no one appeared to be dead, but several people were injured. Charlotte could see her mother tending to them already and watched as her father stared in shock at their own comfortable little home, now without a front wall and half its roof.

"Oh no." Donata stopped beside Charlotte, one hand pressed to her mouth as she took in the destruction the earthquake had caused. "This can't be."

Charlotte frowned. "It's an earthquake. They're rare, but—"

"They can't happen here, though! I know the earth of Fairdale right down to the rock far beneath us, and there's no fault line to be found in it. An earthquake couldn't happen here unless it was forced. And there are precious few witches powerful enough to force something like this...." She looked at Charlotte in dawning comprehension. "It has to be Rozia."

Charlotte found she didn't have the patience for the wise woman's shock—not when she had just warned her about this sort of thing. "Well. Too bad life is such an uncertain proposition, isn't it?" she snapped.

Donata's eyes narrowed balefully. "If Rozia thinks she can get away with this in my village, she's wrong. How dare she invade another witch's territory!"

The anger, at least, was heartening. "Do you think you could get your guild to stop her now?" she asked.

"Is this enough to make them support you against her?"

"I doubt it."

Well, so much for that.

"But..." Donata grabbed Charlotte by the wrist. "I know Rozia. I've known her for more than a century. I know how she thinks, and I know her greatest weakness. If you do as I say, I will help you end her pursuit of King Bruce and possibly even end her time in this kingdom. But you must follow my instructions carefully and not let anyone, not even your lover, dissuade you. Do you understand?"

All the noise in the background faded away as Charlotte's natural sense of determination took hold. "Tell me what to do," Charlotte said firmly. "And I'll make it happen."

33

KING BRUCE

*B*ruce wasn't accustomed to feeling helpless. The hardest thing was to keep himself from overreacting. In his dragon form, he was the biggest, most powerful being in the kingdom, and everyone knew it.

Even as Trieste seemed to be falling to pieces, he had never suffered from the sense that he was failing. He was doing everything he could; it was so much more than most could say. His people knew they could count on him.

At least it had been true until Charlotte's return from Fairdale, arriving in the courtyard with a cart full of lilac bushes and a plea for aid.

"Every house facing the road is damaged terribly," she said after she explained what had occurred there. "Is there any way you can send workers to help them rebuild? Or at least help fund the repairs?"

"Of course," Bruce assured her, pulling her close and wrapping her up in his arms.

Servants bustled around them, unloading the cart, but neither of them paid them any heed.

Charlotte shivered in his grasp, laying her head on his shoulder and muffling her sobs in his shirt.

"I'll get a crew on the road to help them tomorrow and ensure they get the supplies they need to make repairs. Was anyone…fatally injured?"

"No," Charlotte said with a sniffle. "The worst was a broken leg and a head injury during the initial quake. However, parents have had to be quite stern with their children about getting too close to the crevasse. It's nearly ten feet deep." She sighed. "It will take a lot of time and effort to fix this. Do you think…" She looked up at Bruce. "Do you think this happened because of me?"

"It has nothing to do with you," Bruce told her, the honesty of it sinking like a stone into the depths of his soul. "None of this is your fault. Rozia is fixated on me, and her patience is growing thin. She must have seen you with me and decided to act against you because of her jealousy, but none of it is your fault. It's only mine." If only he had never made a bargain with her. If only he had tried harder to escape it or had been more clever and changed the terms of the deal before signing his life over to her. No, what was happening to the kingdom right now was his fault and no one else's.

Charlotte shook her head, then leaned up and kissed his cheek. Bruce turned into her embrace, and the next kiss was full on the lips, ending slowly and sweetly a few moments later. "I'm tired," she said. "I think I'd like to go to bed. In your room, if you don't mind."

"I'll never tire of your company," Bruce assured her.

"Not even when I'm old and gray, and you're still young and handsome?"

Time seemed to slow down for a moment. All the servants, who a moment ago Bruce would have sworn were minding their own business, seemed to be holding their breath, listening in with all their might while pretending they weren't. It was one thing for a commoner like them to have an affair with the king, but it was another thing altogether for her to presume to have a permanent place by his side.

Audacious—Bruce could see that in some people's facial expressions.

Outrageous, some of the more conservative servants seemed to say with their frowns.

"If I'm fortunate enough not to drive you off by then, I'll count myself very blessed," Bruce said, loud enough to be heard by those listening so intently.

He led Charlotte into the castle, away from prying eyes and ears, and into his bedroom, where a meal had been laid out in preparation for her return.

"Thank you." Charlotte only picked at the food. "Aren't you joining me?"

"I've already eaten," he admitted. "Is the food not to your liking?"

She wasn't a picky eater but was averse to some of the more daring dishes, mostly recipes the cooks had collected from faraway lands.

"I'm not that hungry." She yawned. "I'm tired." She yawned again. "I would really like to get in bed."

"Of course, my love."

While Charlotte cleaned up in the adjoining wash-room, Bruce called for a servant to take away the meal, and she came out wearing her nightgown. He helped her settle in bed and lay down beside her.

"My trip started so well," she said ruefully. "Flying with you was the most wondrous experience of my life. I'd love to do it again sometime soon."

"I'll take you anywhere you want to go," Bruce told her. The way he felt right now, he would fly her to the moon and back if she asked him, or at least do his best to make it happen. "Anytime. As long," he amended, "as my abilities aren't needed for the good of Trieste at the time."

"That's perfectly reasonable," Charlotte agreed. "Although, with everything happening lately, I doubt you'll have any time left for gadding about with me. New trouble keeps popping up everywhere, and your help is constantly needed." She turned to her side and propped her head up on one hand. "Actually, I think that it would be a good idea for you to take me with you on your patrols and rescue missions. You don't have a royal historian, and you should have someone to record everything that's been happening lately, not just for posterity. Perhaps seeing it all laid out would give you a better idea of where Rozia might strike next. After all, witches have many powers, but I don't think they can fly, can they? If she's moving around by horse, her mischief is contained to the distance a strong animal could go in one day."

That was a very sound idea, inspired even, except for the way Bruce's heart felt like it would jump out of his throat at the thought of deliberately bringing Charlotte into danger.

Accidentally exposing her in Fairdale had already left him weak in the knees. How would he be able to focus on the task at hand if he was worried sick about her well-being?

She must have seen the uncertainty on his face because she leaned in and kissed him soundly. "I would never demand such a thing of you," she assured him. "But I do think my presence could be helpful. Just tell me you'll consider it."

"I will," Bruce assured her.

He would keep his promise to consider bringing her along, but he doubted that he would do that.

Rozia herself might not be able to fly, but she could use magic to turn into a bird and fly or she could just disappear from one spot and reappear in another.

He had seen her do that.

Her power was incredible, and she was running amok without the witches' guild clipping her wings.

Perhaps alienating the guild hadn't been a smart move on his part.

34

KING BRUCE

*O*ver the next week, as problems in Trieste seemed to keep coming and Bruce was forced to spend long days away from Charlotte, he thought a lot about her proposal.

Most of the turmoil was internal, but eight days after Charlotte returned to him, he was called again to Hariston, where another earthquake had caused his guard tower to topple over entirely. While the stones were still falling, a regiment of armored cavalry had crossed the border from Glorian and laid siege to the town of Hariston.

When Bruce arrived, he was not as kind to the interlopers as he was to the band of stupid youths who had thrown rocks at the tower before. That had been a prank, but as he had suspected, it had been a precursor to a formal attack, mounted against his town in the dead of night when the Glorians knew he wouldn't be able to come to stop them.

Thank the gods, his resident militia was formidable, and even with their tower destroyed, they'd managed to save most of the weapons they had stockpiled there, which included a small grapeshot catapult that they had filled with chunks scavenged from the tower and then fired at the cavalry unit as they'd rode into town.

The horses had scattered, squealing in terror. Men had fallen heavily to the ground, their armor making the trip even more painful than usual.

The people of the town had time to convene in the meetinghouse, the largest and most defensible building outside of the destroyed tower. There they had stayed, fighting against the intruders and ultimately having to watch as their attackers set torches to their houses one by one.

The invaders were so busy setting fires that they hadn't noticed the sunrise. When Bruce arrived, he landed right in front of the meetinghouse, black wings flaring as he roared with fury and might.

The townspeople cheered, and the man who'd led the charge against them pissed himself.

Bruce knew that particular stench quite well.

He lowered his menacing head until he was at eye level with the lord of the Glorian town right across the border. "We meet again," he growled. "Only this time, it's not boys throwing stones. It's men attacking a peaceful town, setting homes on fire, and bringing panic and misery to my people."

"We...we..." The lord swallowed hard. "Trieste is cursed by the gods! Everyone says so! Seeing your tower fall was an invitation from the gods to take back the land that was once ours! You forced us into a treaty forty years ago that was patently unjust and unfair, and—" He squeezed his eyes shut and whimpered in terror as a trail of smoke trickled from Bruce's maw, then began to cough.

"Forty years ago, you and three other nations made a pact to attack and divide Trieste as you saw fit once you killed my family and the men defending my country. You tried to loot us, to pillage us, to destroy us, and you dare to claim that you've been treated unjustly?" Bruce shook his massive head, smoke trailing from his nostrils. "Let us take this to your king and have a parlay with him. I wonder if he shares your opinion."

"Wha... you—no!"

Bruce grabbed the armored lord in his claws, then glared at his soldiers. "If you don't stand down right now, your lord will pay the price. I will take it out of his hide. Throw your weapons down, and then fetch water to put these fires out. Deny me, and I will burn your town to the ground on my way back."

"Obey him!" the frightened lord squeaked in terror. "Do everything the king says!"

His men would have complied even without his

order. Once the townspeople had collected the invaders' weapons and carried them into the meeting-house for safekeeping, Bruce felt comfortable taking off with the damn lord in his clutches.

It would take him about an hour to reach Glorian's capital, and he wasn't looking forward to the flight with the sniveling lord and the stench of urine wafting off him.

His unexpected landing outside the castle of the King of Glorian created quite a stir, especially with the castle staff realizing who he had caged in his claw.

"I demand to meet with your king immediately!" he bellowed.

The castle guards and servants goggled at Bruce. None had been alive when he'd destroyed the Glorian army and defeated the former king. They were used to thinking of him more as a legend than a real being.

When the new king—the son of the man Bruce had defeated—came out to meet him, he appeared both anxious and displeased.

"What is the meaning of this? You're not allowed this far into Glorian."

"Not unless our peace treaty is broken." Bruce released the quivering lord from the cage of his claws. "Tell him what you did," he commanded.

What followed was hours upon hours of explana-tion, bargaining, disagreement, and more writing than Bruce could bear. Treaties had to be updated, and reparations had to be settled ...that part was hard since he didn't have an accurate count of how many homes had burned.

You would know if Charlotte was here.

It would have been a little dangerous, but he could protect her. He hadn't seen her for over an hour of waking time this past week.

Admit it; you miss her and know she could be helpful. Just let her! She wants to be.

The proceedings in Glorian took so long that Bruce barely made it back to Ashelvin before sunset. He landed in the courtyard with a thump, and transformed at a spot already replanted with the lilac bushes that Charlotte had brought back.

She waited for him in the pavilion with a change of clothing, a bowl of food, and, most importantly, a smile.

He'd come to rely on her cheerful greetings to get him through his gloomy days.

"Charlotte," he said before she could ask him about his day. "Come with me next time. I can't promise there won't be dangers, but I'll do everything I can to keep you safe."

Her smile turned into a happy grin. "Thank you." She leaned in and kissed him possessively.

Bruce wrapped his arms around her, torn between gentleness and an urgent, rising need. "I would love to join you," Charlotte said on an exhale as they finally pulled apart. "But now you'd better join me in your quarters. We have time before court is scheduled to begin."

Was she proposing what Bruce thought she was?

He hadn't outright asked, not wanting to take something she wasn't comfortable giving, but...

"I've just had some very special tea," she added, and—yep.

Time for bed.

35

CHARLOTTE

*C*harlotte thought she knew Bruce fairly well at this point. She had been his scribe for months now, his lover for almost as long. He had always been wonderful to her, especially in bed, but this...he was taking her to a new level of pleasure, and he hadn't even undressed yet.

"Ahh!" She crested for the second time, riding the press of his tongue into ecstasy. It wasn't until he pressed a finger inside of her that she remembered that this time was different. He was going to take her and finally claim her fully.

She couldn't wait.

"I'm ready," she breathed, running her hands into his hair to get him to look up at her—he seemed transfixed by the sight of his finger disappearing inside her body. "I'm ready now."

"Give me a moment for caution," Bruce said with a smile as he slid a second finger inside her. She could feel the stretch now, feel how her body shifted and moved to accommodate him. "I want to make sure you enjoy this."

Charlotte laughed. "I'm already enjoying it! I will enjoy it even more when you get inside of me!"

"One more," he coaxed, sliding it into her.

Oh. Oh, that was nice, that was so nice. Three fingers made her feel so full, and the way they moved, rubbed, and slid in her slickness, oh...

Oh gods, she was going to...she was...

Charlotte moaned and closed her eyes as another orgasm washed over her, bathing her body in warmth and spine-tingling pleasure.

How, with just his fingers, she could never...

"No more waiting," she murmured, holding out her arms. "I want you."

"I'm coming," he assured her, moving back just far enough to get his clothes off. Charlotte admired the image her beloved made, so strong and handsome, his body lean and well-muscled from his time spent as a dragon. His shoulders were only as broad as a man's, but most of the time, they carried the weight of the kingdom. Right now, though, they were only a man's, and Charlotte was just as ready as Bruce was to forget every trouble and lose herself to the pleasure, to him, to their future together.

As he finally leaned forward into her grasp, Charlotte pulled him in close until he hovered right at her precipice.

Slowly, smoothly, he began to press inside of her.

Charlotte's eyes widened. This was nothing like the fingers he'd used to bring her to climax before. This was thicker, longer, and more intense than she'd expected. To be touched so deeply, filled so completely….

By the time Bruce was fully inside her, both were panting.

"Are you all right?" he asked stiffly, his jaw clenched tight in his effort to stay still.

Charlotte stared at him for a long moment, real-izing that this was his first time too, or at least the first time in so long that it might as well be a new beginning.

"Yes," she murmured, tilting her head to kiss along that too-tense jaw. "I'm so good I could overflow with it. Are you all right?"

"A bit on edge," he admitted with laughter. "I'm afraid that if I start moving, I'll finish too quickly and leave you wanting."

Now it was Charlotte's turn to laugh. "It's not a contest! And if it was, then clearly, I'm already winning as I've climaxed three times from your masterful attention tonight!" She wrapped her legs around his hips and drew him in tighter. "Show me that you want me. Don't hold back. Everything else can wait."

Bruce sucked in a long breath, then reared up onto his arms. He pulled Charlotte's legs over his shoulders, and looking down at her determinedly, he began to move.

Pinned, claimed, and held by the man she loved, Charlotte could only lie back and feel as Bruce drove into her repeatedly, picking up speed and force until she felt them move up the bed.

Although she'd climaxed not five minutes ago, she could feel the swell of orgasm building inside of her once more. She was so slick yet tight, and his movements inside her were pure pleasure. They could fall right off the bed for all she cared as long as he kept going.

"Yes, yes, yes," Charlotte chanted. "Yes, oh, Bruce, Bruce!"

"Touch yourself," he said, staring down at her avidly.

His cheeks were flushed, his hair completely askew, and his pupils large and dark. He looked hungry like he was on the verge of coming himself. This was her chance to tip over together with him.

Charlotte reached down between their bodies and rubbed all around her clit. It was too sensitive now to touch directly, but the feather-light touches of her fingers were just what she needed to bring her to the precipice and, a second later, to send her right over it.

She screamed—maybe it was Bruce's name, maybe it was a cry to the gods, or maybe it was as inarticulate as she felt. That was the moment Bruce had somehow been holding back for. Thrusting into her a few more times, he finally stopped as deep as he could go and churned his hip as he emptied his seed into her.

Charlotte pulled his body close to hers, clasping him in an embrace she felt down to her toes. They held each other through the aftershocks until Bruce softened enough to dislodge from inside of her.

"Don't ask me if I'm all right," Charlotte said as Bruce opened his mouth.

He chuckled. "You know me so well."

"I do," she said archly before grinning out of sheer satisfaction. "I know you always think of me and my comforts first. This time, trust me, you really don't have to. I'm more than all right." She knew she had to look terribly sappy but couldn't help it. She was in love and would move mountains and fight witches for it.

Speaking of...

"Bruce," she began, curling against his side, "you may be a bit surprised by some of the things I do as we travel together. Please, don't let them get to you, all right? It's all necessary and will help us in the long run."

Despite her efforts at keeping him close and calm, Bruce pushed up onto his elbow and stared at her, his face alarmed. "What are you talking about? Does this have to do with Rozia? Darling, she's dangerous! Don't try anything with her, I beg you."

"It's only indirectly about her," Charlotte promised. "I have no intention of confronting Rozia, I promise." *Although if she chooses to confront me, that's another matter.* "I've found a possible path out of your curse, and I must take it."

"Charlotte." Bruce sounded both intrigued and agonized. "It's not your responsibility to deal with my curse. I'd sooner die than let you get tangled up in this mess with Rozia."

"I know," Charlotte said, nodding, but tears filled her eyes too. "But I have to at least try. Even if Rozia stops tormenting Trieste, if I don't manage to break your curse, I'll still be leaving you alone one day. I just can't bear the thought. You shouldn't have to be alone for the rest of your life!"

She'd thought of making him promise her that he would choose another woman once she was gone, but then he would be going through the same torment again. His only option would be to wed a witch, and he would never do that. Bruce would rather spend eternity alone than marry Rozia or any other witch.

"There is plenty of time to worry about that, my love." He kissed her forehead. "We have many decades ahead of us." His voice broke on the last word, betraying his emotions.

Was he as overwhelmed as she was by their powerful, intimate connection?

"Let me try," she begged. "Just once. I promise that I won't come to any harm. I might seem a bit different when we're out together, but here, in these rooms, I'll always be your Charlotte."

"This is a lot to ask," Bruce said somberly. "You're asking me to trust you, and I do. I trust you with my life, Charlotte. But you're asking me to trust you with your life, and that's so much harder for me." He leaned down and kissed her. "Just be careful and protect yourself, all right?"

"I will," Charlotte promised.

She would do her best to keep that promise, too. Hopefully, Rozia would fall for the act and get curious enough to want to talk.

KING BRUCE

*T*he next morning, Bruce held to his word and brought Charlotte out with him. It was getting cooler in the mornings as summer turned toward autumn, so he made sure she was wearing layers and an extra cloak before taking her into his arms in the courtyard. He held her close to his chest with one arm, stabilizing his enormous body with the other before launching himself aloft. No leaping transformations for him now, not when he had such precious cargo to carry.

No dire emergency required his attention for once, so Bruce took a more leisurely route to the last place where Rozia had wreaked havoc, circling on thermals and treating Charlotte to a bird's eye view of the land far below them. She stared at everything avidly, her writing equipment stuffed into a leather bag that she wore across her chest.

"Where are we?" she called out after half an hour or so of flight.

"Near the western border," Bruce said, careful to modulate his voice so he didn't hurt her ears. "There was an outbreak of plague in a village there two days ago. Their local wise woman rooted it out quickly, but many sick people are still isolated in their homes. I helped haul water for them and helped their neighbors with some of the farming work they would otherwise have attended to." And if he never had to dig furrows in the soil with his claws again, it would be too soon. He still felt the dirt lodged beneath his nails, even multiple baths later.

"Plague, you say?" He could practically hear her mind working. "And before that, it was a village three hours north of there, yes? Another flooding?"

"Flooding which overwhelmed their grain silo. It would have destroyed their stores entirely if we hadn't dried the grain quickly enough."

"Let me guess," she said playfully, "you broke the grain silo in two and spread the lot out on the ground with a few sweeps of your tail."

"It was a bit more involved than that," he groused good-naturedly. Although honestly, Bruce had just tipped the damn thing over and shaken the grain onto the tarps the villagers had laid out. From there, the sun did the rest of the work.

"Do they realize it, d'you think?"

"Does who realize what?"

"Do your people realize how lucky they are to have you to help them with such things?" Charlotte said in perfect earnestness.

"I like to think so," Bruce said, then sighed. "Of course, many of them might also realize that they wouldn't have some of these problems if it weren't for me."

He could barely feel her gentle pat-pat on the scales of his claw, but he appreciated it, nonetheless. "The only reason they'd have fewer problems because of you is if they had died back in the war," she said. "I think more people realize that than you know."

"I appreciate the—" Bruce paused and squinted into the distance. Was that...yes, a trail of black smoke was rising from the ground, large enough that it had to be more than someone burning trash. "We've got trouble," he growled, then pumped his wings hard to pick up speed. Charlotte didn't make any sounds of distress, but he held her a little closer than he had before as he hurried to the aid of yet another town that had fallen victim to Rozia's sabotage campaign.

Bruce landed a good hundred yards from the town, where some children were standing and staring at the fire with their minders, mostly older women and men. The younger adults were swarming the source of the fire, a building right in the center of town. "Stay out here," Bruce told Charlotte as he let her down.

She didn't respond, which was odd. Even odder was how she refused to meet his eyes, just nodded and clutched her satchel to her chest. Bruce didn't have the time to let it bother him or ask what was wrong with her, not when he had a town to save. He eased his body down their main street, careful not to do any more damage, and surveyed the site of the fire.

The building was large and burning hotly, too hot for the people hauling water to be able to put out. But these houses were all thatch and wood, with only a bit of stone for support here and there. If he flapped his wings to smother this fire, he might blow half the other ones over.

"My king!" A soot-stained man ran up to him, his posture half pleading, half hoping. "Please, is there anything you can do for us? If the fire spreads, we could lose the entire town!"

Bruce could only think of one thing to try. "Keep everyone well back and be ready to work fast to put out anything that might fall," he ordered, and the man shouted out his orders even as he ran to get out of harm's way.

Bruce knew he would only have one chance to get this done. He took measurements in his mind, calculated the best spots for his claws, then leaped into the air, allowing his wings to billow out and slow his fall just enough to leave him time to grab the house. With his claws sunk into the bases of each corner, he flew back up into the air with the house. Not just part of it but the entire structure.

It was hard. Not just because of the added load he was lifting but because Bruce still had to be careful not to use too much force for fear of doing even more damage. By the time he got the burning house beyond the town's limits and set it down in a deserted field where it could do no more harm, the fire had managed to singe even his thick, strong scales in places. Bruce stepped back gingerly from the blaze. "No, no," he told one man who ran forward with a bucket. "It's too late."

The man dropped his burden, then fell to his knees and wept. "My family's home," he cried out. "It existed for generations, and now it's nothing, nothing. Where will we stay? What will we do?"

"Be thankful for your lives," Bruce said snappishly, not meaning to sound so harsh. He was wounded and worried about Charlotte, and the day had just begun. "Homes may be rebuilt but lives once lost are lost forever."

"Wise words," the sooty man who had initially greeted Bruce said as he ran in, putting one arm around the fallen man's shoulders. "Never fear, Eben. We'll all help you build it back, aye? And you and the children can stay with me and Liv until it's done."

"I lost her portrait," Eben wept, too overwhelmed to respond to logic. "My Sarra's portrait, the only thing I had left to remember her by. It's gone and burned, burned, my poor lost Sarra...."

Bruce had never felt so out of place in all his life. "Is

there anything else that troubles you?" he asked the sooty man.

"No, your Majesty." The man straightened up and bowed. All around him, the rest of the people bowed, but almost none met his eyes. "You saved almost all of our homes today, sire, and would have saved this one, too, were it possible. Thank you for your aid."

Bruce nodded stiffly. "Be well." Then he turned and walked back through the town, careful on his burned feet, until he got to Charlotte and the others again. She had been talking animatedly to a group of children right before he arrived but went silent as soon as he got close. Why? Was this part of her strange plan to help him break the curse? If so, he didn't understand it in the slightest.

"Time to leave," he said, holding out a clawed forepaw to her.

Charlotte gasped when she saw the damage but came quickly and settled into his grasp. Even though it hurt, Bruce felt better once he had her close again. He took off, and once they were well above the village, Charlotte finally exclaimed, "We need to get back to Ashelvin and treat your wounds right now!"

"There's no point." There never was. "They'll be much better as soon as I change shape again. Damage taken in one form doesn't tend to stick around through the transformation."

"But that's no reason for you to suffer now," Charlotte pointed out. "We could—"

"Is it part of your plan to make yourself seem distant from me?" Bruce asked bluntly. "If so, that plan will be less effective if the entire castle's staff sees you fussing over me."

Charlotte was quiet for a moment, and Bruce wondered whether or not he'd offended her. He was just about to apologize when she said, "No, you're right, that won't do. But we could find an isolated stream or river, and you could at least bathe your wounds in it for a while. It would be cooling, and no one would be able to see me fussing over you then. Which I fully plan to do, by the way."

Despite his own instinct to mope, Bruce felt his mood lightening. "That would be…acceptable."

Charlotte laughed. "I'm so glad you think so, darling. Now, let's look for a likely river where you can settle in for a foot bath. Hmm, probably a muddy bottom is best, don't you agree? Pebbles might irritate the wounds—the gods know I wouldn't want to be stepping on rocks if I'd just burned my feet raw. What about the Resteen? It's close to this part of the country, right? And I seem to remember reading reports about needing to dredge it in certain shallow sections whenever…."

Bruce, buoyed by Charlotte's conversation and her delightful use of the word "darling" when referring to him, which completely erased the negative feelings he had associated with the word after the witch used it, flew toward the Resteen River in a much better mood than he'd been in moments ago.

She transforms everything about me for the better. Even if she can't find a way to change me back, I'll never push her away.

No matter what things looked like along the way.

CHARLOTTE

*T*he tenor of Charlotte and Bruce's days was set after that first outing together.

They left the castle together every morning, honing in on the likeliest spot of trouble, judging from where it had popped up. Nine times out of ten, they were right, and Bruce was able to forestall terrible damage and save lives along the way.

Not that their system was perfect, as attested to when a bridge collapsed fifty miles from where they'd flown to. But even then, Bruce got word of it quickly enough and did everything he could to mitigate the damage.

The constant, heavy work wore on him, though. Charlotte could see the changes it wrought in the hollowing of his cheeks and the dark circles that popped up under his eyes. It didn't help that as soon as he set down anywhere and let her go, Charlotte immediately behaved as though she didn't want to be there. Oh, she worked with the townspeople and took notes, keeping track of every facet of the incidents with a scribe's attention to detail, but she never let herself look happy about it, and she never came back to Bruce before he summoned her.

It was terrible for both of them, and she did her best to alleviate the effects of her forced distancing as soon as they were alone again. She could tell that Bruce was close to asking her "why" a few times, and if he had asked...well if he had asked, she would have told him. She hoped to be spared that necessity, though if Rozia didn't reach out soon, she would have to take steps.

They needed to do something.

Something to set the witch off, to push her over the edge instead of constantly being pushed by her while she watched and plotted from afar.

The answer to what that thing might be came to Charlotte two days before the Harvest Festival, after a grueling season of disaster and recovery, disaster and recovery, and careening all over Trieste to handle emergency after emergency with no relief.

It couldn't go on like that. Charlotte couldn't bear to see Bruce get worse day by day as the weight of everything bearing down on him became crushing.

"Bruce," she said that night as they lay in bed together. "I think you should ask me to marry you."

There was a long silence, then—Bruce began to

laugh. He laughed long and hard, so hard that Charlotte wondered if she'd bumped him over the edge into hysteria.

"It's not funny!" she insisted, although she was having difficulty holding her laughter back.

"Not—not what you s-said, but how you said it," Bruce managed. "No hinting, no asking me to marry you, just outright telling me that I need to ask y-you to marry—" He began to howl again. Charlotte was forced to biff him with a heavy down pillow to get him to stop.

"Is the thought of being married to me so awful?" she joked.

"You know it's not," Bruce said, sitting up and wiping his eyes with the edge of the pillow she'd hit him with. "Of course, it's not. I would love to be married to you, but..." He looked at her keenly. "That's not what you said, is it? You didn't say you wanted to be married to me. You said I need to ask you to marry me."

"Yes," Charlotte agreed.

"Very specific, love."

"I know."

"What are you planning?"

"I'd rather not say," she said—at least she could be honest about her dishonesty. "But I think it's vital that we at least make people think we will be married soon. You could announce it at the Harvest Festival. That way, word will really spread fast."

The quicker it spread, the faster Rozia would hear of it. If there was anything that would tip her over the edge at this point, it had to be the thought of Bruce marrying someone else when she wanted so desperately to be made queen.

Bruce reached out and took her hand. "Would you like to be queen?"

"I want to be with you," Charlotte replied. "For as long as I possibly can, no matter what title we put on our relationship. I will stay with you whether we are married or not."

Bruce smiled. "Then I'll make the announcement at the Harvest Festival. Be prepared for a lot of questions from people in the castle, though. They're rather protective of you these days. They might try to talk you out of it."

"No one who really knows me would ever try to change my mind on something so vital to me." Not that a few hadn't already tried, but they were either fearmongers or several comely maids who figured if the king was going to slum it with a servant, it might as well be them. "Thank you, Bruce. I promise it's going to all make sense soon."

"I believe you." He leaned over and kissed her, and soon there was no more talk between them, just the language of bodies finding pleasure in each other. And then gratified and exhausted sleep.

True to his word, Bruce made the announcement of their wedding at the Harvest Festival in front of a huge crowd, as nearly everyone in the capital was attending. "I want you all to celebrate this momentous occasion with us," he said to dumbfounded cheers and squawks of astonishment. "I never thought the day would come that Trieste would have a queen again, but my bride-to-be has exceeded all my expectations." He held out his hand to Charlotte, and she joined him on the platform, stiff in her new finery and smiling for him but dropping it as soon as he wasn't looking at her.

Let them see my hesitation. Let them read me as inexperienced and afraid. Let the right person—or the wrong person, really—take the bait.

Looking out at the massive crowd with trepidation and fierce determination in her heart, Charlotte could only hope her ruse would work.

CHARLOTTE

*T*he day after the Harvest Festival, Bruce was called to aid a town a hundred miles east of Ashelvin. It was a long flight, and upon arrival they saw the issue was a massive rockslide that had destroyed half the buildings there. He set her firmly beyond the bounds of the town and the mountain itself.

"Stay safe and be careful," he said before heading into the town to help move the largest boulders and clear rubble to facilitate the search for survivors.

Charlotte felt sick watching him go. This was one of the worst disasters yet, and quite likely the deadliest. She let her ill feelings rise to the surface, turning away from the town and clutching her bag to her chest like a touchstone as she trembled and shook, imagining the surprise and pain of the people trapped within their homes as the rocks began to fall...

Stomp, stomp, stomp... Was it another avalanche? No, this was too regular, and it stopped almost as soon as Charlotte detected it.

"It's just all so terrible, isn't it?"

Charlotte lifted her head so fast she got a crick in her neck. "Who's there?" she said sharply.

A woman stepped out from behind a nearby tree, a tree that shouldn't have been wide enough to hide her. Behind it, Charlotte could just make out the shape of a cottage that hadn't been there before.

More magic from Rozia.

So...this was the witch who had done so many terrible things in the name of power.

Charlotte stared at her in disgust. She was as beautiful as twilight with that long dark hair and exquisite face, but she seemed just as distant and cold.

She needed to break down the distance between them and make the witch feel like she was in control.

Charlotte shrank in on herself. "You...you're the...the..."

"The person who can save you from a king you clearly despise and an engagement you don't seem to want?" Rozia smiled. "Oh yes, little girl, I can be your savior. I can spirit you far, far away from King Bruce, dirty old brute that he is, and put you someplace he will never be able to find you."

Charlotte shook her head. "No, you can't."

Rozia laughed. "Do you think there's anything that dragon king of yours can do that I can't easily counter?

Look at how I've had him running around his kingdom like a fool all summer. I can free you from him."

By stabbing me in the back, I'm sure.

"It's not that simple," Charlotte said.

"And why not?"

Now she needed to play things so, so carefully. Charlotte tightened her arms around her satchel and prayed that Donata's plan worked. "I'm...bound to him," Charlotte explained, her voice just a bit above a whisper. "By magic."

Rozia looked at her sharply. A green light rose in her eyes, illuminating them for a moment like a cat's at night. The glow went away just as quickly, and she scoffed, "Ridiculous. No witch has laid any spell on you, and no other witch would dare lay a spell over any of mine."

"Not witch magic. Scribe magic."

"Scri—there's no such thing as scribe magic!"

Charlotte sighed. "Everything has magic. You should know that. You draw your magic from the earth. Is it so hard to believe that others might also learn to draw magic from the things they are connected to? I only knew the tiniest bits about scribe magic before I got to the castle, but once I was there...." She shuddered. "I learned why King Bruce got rid of his last scribe after having him create one final document for him."

Rozia's eyes narrowed. "A document that does what, exactly?"

"It's a marriage contract, binding whoever signs it to King Bruce. I didn't know what I was signing at first, I swear!" Charlotte insisted, tears rising up in her eyes. "I can't imagine a scribe would be so cruel…the last one must have been forced to write this out before Bruce killed him!"

"Killed him?" Rozia took a step closer. "Really?"

"Yes! That's why scribe magic is so rare—you either build it up by writing the same contract over and over and over again, hundreds or thousands of times, or you charge the contract with an act of brutality like murder."

"Fascinating." The witch seemed truly fascinated, as though she was already picturing the havoc she could wreak by sacrificing even more lives for her cause. "How exactly does this contract bind you to King Bruce? I need details."

"I…you could look at it if you want?" Charlotte offered meekly. "I've been carrying it with me in the hopes that I'd come across someone who could help me undo it, but the only moments I get apart from him are when we're…well." She gestured at the devastated town.

Rozia's smile showed too many teeth.

Hungry bitch.

"Let me see it," she said.

Charlotte reached into the satchel crushed against

her chest and carefully pulled out a piece of parchment. Even to her untrained eyes, it shimmered with magical energy. "Here," she said, holding it out to Rozia.

Rozia took it avidly, looking at both sides and even sniffing it a time or two. "This magic... it's almost familiar. Just the tiniest bit off from what a witch might do."

"Is it?" Charlotte asked. "I suppose even magic has its limits. But please, take a look at the wording—the terms of this contract can only be met once the signatory is equal to the king. That must mean I've got to marry him!"

"Not necessarily," Rozia purred. "There are many different ways to be equal to someone."

Now it was Charlotte's turn to scoff. "Not in the eyes of the law," she said bitterly. "It may look as though King Bruce has made advancements in the equality of the sexes over the years, but the truth is that those are practically meaningless in the actual court of law. I would know. I've been working as his scribe for months now. No, it's marriage or nothing."

"Magic is a more powerful force than the mere joining of two people in matrimony," Rozia declared. "As King Bruce has a powerful magic spell upon him, it stands to reason that you must also be magical to meet the contract terms without having to marry him."

"But I don't have magic!" Charlotte wailed.

"Oh, my dear. Your plight just breaks my heart."

Rozia pressed a hand to her ample chest. "It would be my pleasure to give you enough magic to make you the equal of King Bruce so long as you then swear to me that you will never marry him."

Charlotte's heart pounded in her chest. "Are you saying...you can fulfill the contract for me? Get me out of this marriage?"

"I wouldn't have it any other way," Rozia replied.

"Then..." Charlotte stiffened her spine. This was it. There was no going back after this. "I accept."

"Excellent!" Rozia clapped her hands. "Come here, my dear." Charlotte came to her, then stiffened as Rozia wove her cold, sharp fingers into Charlotte's hair. "Now try to relax," she murmured, flecks of glimmering gold appearing in her eyes. "This might hurt a bit."

"It wi—*aaah!*" It didn't hurt a bit. It burned like her blood had been set on fire. Charlotte writhed and screamed, unable to help herself, but Rozia didn't let go. Magic coursed through her body, filling her, expanding her, making her grow out and up until finally, finally the spell was done.

CHARLOTTE

*C*harlotte slowly opened her eyes. Her vision was blurry at first, but she could just about make out Rozia's outline in front of her. She blinked, and there was the witch in more detail, hunched over her face like a crone.

Rozia looked...older, worn out, as though this magical deal had taken more than just power from her, but life as well.

Donata warned me that might happen.

If it had, Charlotte might be afforded the greatest chance of all. She pushed slowly to her feet, only realizing how tall this new body was when she stood up as tall as two Rozias.

"You...made me a dragon?" Charlotte lifted one massive foot and stared in awe at it.

Her claws were as sharp as daggers and about as long. She felt strong, like she could crush a rock just by squeezing it. Her scales were the most beautiful midday-sky blue she had ever seen. She went to stretch, and a shuddering against her back made her react with instinct, spreading enormous wings out into the air.

Wings. She had her own wings now! She could fly, and she was strong, and she could be the partner that Bruce deserved!

Below her, Rozia cackled. "There!" she said with shrill glee. "Now you are his equal and equally cursed to live as woman and dragon for all time! You shall never marry him, and there's nothing left about you that he could want either." She grabbed the magical parchment that had fallen to the ground and shredded it to bits.

"And now he's safe from you, too," Charlotte replied. She stretched again, feeling her strength and reveling in her newfound power. Power enough to resist a witch's last attacks, perhaps. "Now I can be with him without fear."

Rozia scowled at her. "What do you mean? Nothing is binding you two together, but he still holds a contract with me. He must give me his firstborn if he wants his curse lifted."

"His firstborn," Charlotte agreed. "But a child only legally belongs to its father if the parents are married. If we have a child together while unwed, then that child will take my name, not his."

Rozia gnashed her teeth together. Her beauty

seemed to be crumbling more with every passing second. "You're not pregnant."

"No, I'm not." Although now, at least, she wouldn't have to fear it. "I was never bound by scribe magic either."

The witch's jaw dropped. "You lie."

"Nope." Charlotte's tail swished merrily, knocking over a few little bushes. *Oops!* "There's no such thing as scribe magic! I lied about that part, yeah, but I'm not lying now. That parchment was painted with a potion to make it look impressive, but it was never magical enough to bind me to anyone."

"Then...then our contract is null and void!" She raised her hands. "I'll take the magic back from you, then kill you for your deceit!"

"You entered into the contract without verifying the details," Charlotte pointed out. "The same way you tricked Bruce all those years ago. And I don't think the magic is happy about it. Look at yourself."

For the first time, Rozia seemed to realize something was wrong with her. When she saw the spotting on the backs of her hands, she screamed in terror. "What...what..."

"You've been casting very grandiose spells lately," Charlotte went on, digging her claws into the dirt to keep herself from reaching out and crushing Rozia with them. "The earth has given you great power but gotten very little back apart from misery. A friend of mine said the odds were good that if you spent yourself on a massive spell like, oh, transforming a person into a dragon without getting anything back, the earth might just take away your ability to do magic." Charlotte shook her head. "You betrayed your connection to your own power. Now it's taking what you owe."

"No!" Rozia clapped her hands together, trying to build up her power. There was no flare of light in her eyes this time, though. Her body kept bending, shriveling until, at last, she was nothing more than an ancient hag curled up in a ball on the ground, fighting for every breath.

"*Noooo*," Rozia mewled. She stared uncomprehendingly at Charlotte. "This...you...trickery, deceit. I'll kill...I'll kill..." She tried to reach for Charlotte, her fingers little more than barren twigs covered by a thin veneer of papery skin, but that was the moment her heart gave out. She collapsed for the last time, exhaled dust, and the next moment...

There was nothing left of her but a pile of ragged cloth and the nubbins of what must have been teeth.

Charlotte took a deep breath—a deep, deep breath in her current body. She stared down at the remains of Rozia for a long moment, then tentatively touched them with the tip of a claw.

Nothing. The witch truly was dead. She had done it.

She had done it!

Unbidden, a roar of triumph rose up in Charlotte's chest. She closed her eyes, tilted her head back, and

lifted her voice to proclaim victory. She'd saved everyone! She'd defeated the witch! She'd—

"CHARLOTTE! NOOOO!" That voice was as loud
as her own, and it sounded utterly agonized.

Charlotte turned just in time to face Bruce lunging
forward, claws extended as he pinned her fiercely to
the ground, jaws snapping just above her neck.

KING BRUCE

*B*ruce had never known that he could feel so desperate. One moment he'd been hard at work in the town, moving heaps of debris as delicately as he could just in case life lingered within the rubble, and then he'd heard a titanic roar, the roar of a great beast. He had known it had something to do with Charlotte.

She was in danger. He'd left her alone outside the town, and now—

Seeing the bright blue dragon rise in triumph set fire to his brain, frying every link he had to reason and humanity. He could smell Charlotte, but he could also smell death, and with his Charlotte nowhere to be seen, he could only assume that this dragon, wherever it had come from, had taken her.

Taken her.

His Charlotte.

The woman he loved more than life itself.

He screamed. He didn't know exactly what he roared, but every part of his body was set on taking his despair and fury out on the creature before him. He hit the enemy dragon with all his strength, opened his maw to attack, and—

"Bruce!"

That...wait.

That was Charlotte's voice. And it was coming from...coming from...the dragon?

Bruce was able to stop his attack, but it left him frozen, unable to comprehend what was going on. Where was she?

"It's me," the dragon said, gently now that he was no longer trying to take its—her—head off. "It's me, Charlotte."

"But..." It couldn't be. Could it? "How is this possible?" he asked hoarsely. "How can you be Charlotte?"

"It was Rozia's doing. She—"

Rozia!

Of course, that witch was behind this. Bruce immediately got off Charlotte and inhaled deeply, searching for that foul rose stench. There was only the slightest hint of it in the air, and it was mixed with that musty, deathlike smell that had alarmed him so badly.

"She's gone," Charlotte explained, quiet and slow,

clearly trying her best to calm him down. "Her magic finally turned on her. She made too many bad deals."

Bruce was confounded. He looked at Charlotte, looked deep into her eyes, and scanned her dragonish face to ensure he wasn't under some sort of spell or illusion. "Is it really you?" he asked quietly.

"You had toasted bread with cheese for dinner last night," she said immediately. "And I said that was the sort of thing kids ate for dinner, and you said it was comforting and that I ought to try it before passing judgment, and you were right, it was so nice, so I had the same thing, and we sent the foie gras back to the kitchen. We had apple tarts with sweet cream and a drizzle of honey for dessert, and you said you wouldn't mind drizzling a little honey on my—"

"All right." Yep, it was her. "But…how did she make you a dragon? Why did she make you a dragon?"

Charlotte explained how she had tricked Rozia into believing she was looking for a way out of their relationship and had caused Rozia to overextend herself. "A witch I consulted with believed that Rozia was on the verge of getting rejected by the earth because she drew too much power without giving enough back. She was making bad deals that didn't involve equal exchange left and right, and the one she made with me was the biggest and finally tipped the scales. The earth took what it was due from her."

Bruce was dumbfounded. "How are you so clever?"

"Oh." Charlotte lowered her head bashfully. He

knew she would have blushed if she could have done so in this body. "Well, it really wasn't all that clever, and I wouldn't have known about it if not for the wise woman. But I figured out how to trick Rozia into overextending herself on my own. I just needed to apply a little pressure in the right way, and it wasn't difficult to figure out the witch's weak points. A woman who's gone to such awful lengths to become queen would do anything to keep us from getting married, and she also wanted to hurt me in the process, so...yeah. Now I'm under the same 'curse' you are." She looked up at him with shining eyes. "That means I will live as long as you do, and you might never get rid of me. I hope you're all right with that."

Oh, gods. She was right. If Charlotte was like him now, he would never have to worry about her growing old while he remained frozen in time. He would never have to anticipate the pain of a day when death parted them because of her old age. It was the most incredible blessing he could have ever imagined. "You're brilliant," Bruce told her. "I love you, and since nothing is standing in our way now, I would love to be married to you and make you my queen."

"Of course I—"

"But first." He nodded toward the town behind them. "We have a duty to attend to. Once we're done there, we can speak more of the future." He nudged beneath her long, beautiful jaw with his own, a gentle, dragonish kiss. "You'll need to learn to fly, for starters."

"Oh! Yes, I—yes, let's do that."

Clearing the rest of the rubble went much faster with another set of claws once Bruce assured the townspeople that, yes, this dragon was actually his fiancée and no, she wasn't going to eat them.

She was beyond beautiful in this form, serpentine and elegant. Bruce's heart swelled with joy seeing the admiration on his people's faces as they watched Charlotte work.

Charlotte, in true-to-herself form, didn't even notice them watching her. She dedicated all her attention to the task at hand. When she managed to rescue two small children from a cellar beneath a house that had crumbled above them, everyone cheered her.

By the time they were done, there was just enough daylight left to make it back to the castle. "Are you ready?" Bruce asked, leading her to a field several hundred yards from the village.

"Ready to fly?" She sounded incredibly excited, and the tip of her tail practically vibrated with how fast it flipped back and forth. "Yes! What do I need to do?"

"The most important thing," he began, leaning in and giving her another dragon kiss, "is to trust yourself. Your body knows what to do, even if working out the details will take a while. I literally threw myself off a cliff to learn. Let yourself go, don't be afraid, and follow me."

"That sounds pretty complicated to me," Charlotte said.

"It'll feel far more natural once you're up in the air, I promise. Now. Get your wings moving." Bruce began to beat his immense wings, stirring up dry grass around them. "Pump hard—it takes more than you think to get off the ground! And when you feel ready —jump up!" He leaped into the air, working hard with his wings until he found a thermal to help him rise. Below him, Charlotte was staring up in half-wonder, half-apprehension.

"Go for it!" Bruce called down to her. "Try!"

So much dust and debris rose in the air as she flapped and flapped that Bruce lost sight of Charlotte for a while. He was preparing to go back down and get her when all of a sudden—

"*Aaaahhhhh!*" She sped past him, moving so quickly her wings couldn't even feel the air current he was riding. "I'm *flyiiiing!* Bruce! I'm flying... I'm flying too fast, help me!"

Laughing, he wheeled around and went after her, showing her how to coast and glide before she wore herself out entirely. A little breathless, Charlotte stared at him with tears of wonder in her huge dragon eyes.

"Other than falling in love with you, this is the best thing that's ever happened to me," she said.

Bruce felt the shackles of the curse he'd been carrying for forty years fall away from his heart. For the first time, he felt like he thought she did—incredibly lucky to ride the skies like this with the one he loved.

"I feel the same," he said at last. "Come on, let's head back home. We should both be able to fit in the court-yard if we snuggle close for the landing."

"Show me," Charlotte said eagerly.

And Bruce did.

CHARLOTTE

Their wedding was held in the evening, three full months after the Harvest Festival. It took that long to prepare everything and to make all the people in Trieste aware that the king's fiancée had also been turned into a dragon, and, yes, they were happy about it.

No one batted an eyelid at the dragon part, at least not in the castle. Instead, Charlotte was inundated with congratulations and support, everyone ecstatic over her good fortune.

"However did you do it?" people asked time and again. "How did you convince the witch to transform you? Did she have a change of heart?"

"Something like that," Charlotte replied, not wanting to damage the reputation of the witches' guild.

After all, Donata had helped her pull off this feat,

and the last thing Charlotte wanted was to repay a good deed with a poor one. She also worked on mending the relationship between Bruce and the witches' guild.

After all, it wasn't fair to punish all witches for the deeds of one bad apple.

Trieste met the news of a dragon queen with happiness, and all its neighbors met it with resignation.

Without Rozia stirring up trouble on the borders and in every other town and village in the country, by the time their wedding day arrived everything was, for a wonder, prepared.

Charlotte wore a dress worthy of her new status, and everyone from her parents to her former instructors to Donata herself was there to watch her and Bruce make their vows. The food was incredible and distributed far and wide by the castle kitchen staff to encourage the people of Ashelvin to celebrate along with them.

Once they exchanged vows, the celebration lasted into the early morning with music, fireworks, and cheer gladdening every heart.

Charlotte and Bruce hardly saw any of that. Instead, once the feast was done and they'd been congratulated by the people closest to them, they made their way to their suite and collapsed onto their bed with matching heartfelt sighs.

"Thank goodness that's over," Bruce remarked.

Charlotte knew to take that the way he meant it instead of how it sounded. "So much planning," she agreed. "So many people to consult. If I never see another spreadsheet, it'll be too soon."

Bruce reached over and touched her hand, winding their fingers together. "You love spreadsheets," he teased.

"Mmm, true, I've a weakness for papers with tabs and color-coded inks," Charlotte agreed with a giggle. "And you're not immune to the planning bug yourself, Mr. Seating Chart. How many iterations did you go through to make sure that everyone had a place?"

"Two."

"Bruce."

"Fine, twelve, but they deserve it! The castle staff has been our strongest supporters! It's not right for them to have to spend a day they've worked so hard for on the sidelines, serving others. A rotating seating chart and schedule was the best way to make sure everyone got a moment to relax."

"I know," Charlotte said, squeezing her husband's fingers.

Her husband, oh, her husband.

They were married now. Which was good, given what she had to share. "Um…so."

"So." Bruce rolled over so that he was beside her, then leaned in and kissed her lips. "Have you been feeling better? I know you've been under the weather these past few weeks, despite how you tried to keep it from me."

Oh, he had noticed. That was good. That would make things easier. "Not exactly under the weather," she said. "More like...expecting."

"Expecting what?"

Charlotte rolled her eyes. "Bruce, sweetheart... I'm expecting." She took their joined hands and placed them on her stomach. "We're expecting."

"We're..." He looked down at her abdomen, then back up at her with wide eyes. "What?"

"Expecting. We have an arrival impending. Um, my breadbasket is full? I'm baking something in my oven? I'm up the duff?"

Bruce went pale, then bright red. "Are you serious? This is not one of your jokes, right? Because it's not funny."

Did he think she would joke about a thing like that?

"Of course, I'm serious!" She patted the back of his hand. "You're going to be a father. Congratulations."

"I..."

Oh dear. Was he actually not happy about this?

They hadn't discussed having children, but the pregnancy hadn't been planned. She'd only missed her tea the one time, and that was because they'd changed back to their human forms too far out to make it to the castle.

Nevertheless, Charlotte thought the fact that they

would have a child was awesome. What could be better than expanding their circle of love to include a little Bruce or a little Charlotte?

Did he not agree?

Was he afraid that the child would be born a dragon?

That was possible, but would it be so bad?

All of a sudden, her arms were full of Bruce, her mouth completely covered by his as he kissed her passionately, laughing and almost sobbing at times. "I never thought," he said between kisses, "that I would be a father. I never thought I could be, not with Rozia's threats hanging over my head. But you, clever, wonderful woman, beautiful and glorious star of stars, have changed everything for me. Everything." He pulled back so she could see his whole face and his loving, awestruck expression. "I adore you, and I will adore our child. I can't wait to be a father and for you to be a mother."

They kissed again, all the stress of the long day dissolving into a blissful mist, and just as warmth and happiness overtook Charlotte completely...

BRUCE

*I*t was like coming out of the best dream Bruce could remember. Better, because he remembered everything that had happened in the virtual world with crisp clarity instead of the immediate forgetfulness he always felt after waking up from a dream.

Bruce blinked at the ceiling, amazed at how relaxed and happy he felt. He was even smiling, for heaven's sake. Smiling, and he'd only been awake for two seconds. Had he been smiling while he'd been under?

He didn't care if the tech had seen him smiling like a fool. That had been the best time of his life, bar none, and he owed a big thank you to Peter and the rest of the gang for setting him up to do this.

"I guess you had a good time," his tech said beside him as he took the IV line out of Bruce's hand. "Was it as fun as you had expected?"

"It was much more than I could have ever imagined," Bruce said. "It was incredible." He didn't even mind the pinch of the needle as it disengaged from the back of his hand. "I can't believe how amazing my partner was. I mean, the person that created that fantasy must be so talented."

"Yeah? Were you the werewolf of your dreams?"

Bruce grinned. "Even better. I got to be a dragon." And he didn't mind that, instead of a hairy chest, he had scales in the adventure.

He'd gotten to fly! To spread his wings and soar through the sky. What could be better than that?

Being a dragon beat being a werewolf any day.

"Dude." The tech looked impressed. "That's so cool."

"I know. I spent a lot of time as a dragon, and it all felt so natural. I never doubted for one second that I was this huge flying reptile who could breathe fire." Bruce shook his head. "I can see why people come back and do this again and again. If I could go flying right now, I would."

Who needed real life when the fantasy was so much better?

"You can, you know," the tech said as he wound up the cords and went to get Bruce's shoes. "You can do it again, I mean. You can always book another Experience here."

Bruce seriously considered it.

He'd been skeptical about the whole thing only hours ago. Wow, that was unbelievable. He'd lived months in the fantasy while only three hours had passed in the real world.

Coming to the studios had been a way to forget his woes for a few hours and also to make his friends happy. Now, though…now he couldn't even remember what his woes had been before he'd gotten into the Experience.

But, and here was the kicker, he wanted to do it again with Charlotte or whoever she was in real life. He already knew that the fantasy she'd created had given him some of the most fun of his entire life. The connection he'd felt with her…that had seemed so much more real than anything he had ever experienced.

Don't be an idiot and fall in love with someone you can't have.

But maybe he could have her, at least as a partner for more Experiences. It would be costly, but the way he felt now, he would sell his most prized guitar to do this again. Not that he needed to. Bruce had enough money saved up to afford to splurge on many virtual vacations. But if he hadn't, he would have done it.

"Is it possible to request the same person for another Experience?" Bruce asked.

"Of course! It's encouraged, even." He smiled. "After all, we promise to find our clients their perfect matches. It's only natural that they would want to spend more time with that person." The tech shrugged. "That being said, some people are addicted to having a variety of partners, and they don't want to partner with anyone more than once." He looked into Bruce's eyes. "I can tell that you're not one of those. You want your perfect match lady, and no one else."

Brian was either very perceptive, or he had seen it happen hundreds of times before.

The thing was, Bruce wanted to meet the real Charlotte. Was that even possible?

He hadn't read all the small print of the release he had signed, and he'd been so anxious to start the adventure that he had listened with only half an ear to his Experience coordinator.

You'll never know unless you ask.

Bruce took a deep breath. "What about meeting the person I was matched with outside of the Experience? Is that possible?"

The tech smiled knowingly. "You can put in a request. Many clients do that, but not everyone who comes here is interested in a face-to-face meeting. If she doesn't want to meet you, we need to respect her wishes. We will not release her information. We don't want our clients to get stalked by their Experience partners."

"I understand. No stalking," Bruce agreed quickly.

He couldn't imagine wanting to make someone that uncomfortable. If he reached out and was told no, of course he would respect that.

But if there was even a chance that she'd say yes to

just exchanging emails, he could at least chat with her about the sort of Experience they wanted to have next.

If she wanted another Experience with him.

Screw it.

I had a great time, I think she did too, and I will ask. "What do I need to do to reach out to her?"

"You can use the messaging system associated with your Perfect Match account," his tech said, pulling up a new screen on the computer beside Bruce's chair. "Here, I'll show you how to get in. Then, when you're ready, you can check if your partner is interested in... whatever you guys want to talk about. If she doesn't respond, though, don't try to reach her again."

"Thank you," Bruce said. He was genuinely grateful for the help, but what he really needed right now was luck. If he was going to pull off meeting the woman who'd literally made his dreams come true, he was going to need it.

43

MONA

*M*ona woke up feeling like she was floating on a cloud. She honestly couldn't remember ever being quite so blissed out before, not even during some unfortunate experimentation in college that she'd never told anyone about.

The virtual Experience had been everything she'd hoped for and so much more. They had taken her story and expanded on it, branched out in directions she hadn't imagined. Had it been the artificial intelligence running the simulation, or had it been her brain and that of her partner pushing the limits of her initial creativity with their collaboration and taking the adventure in unexpected directions?

"You look like you had a nice time," Leann said pleasantly as she started detaching the wires connecting Mona to the machines.

"It was incredible," she gushed. "I'm honestly, like,

two seconds away from calling my mother and thanking her for getting me the gift certificate in the first place, which I swore I would never do because then she gets ideas, y'know? But I really do feel wonderful. I wish I could go back already."

"That's fantastic." Leann smiled. "You know, you could always request to meet your Experience partner in real life. Maybe he would be willing to do another session with you."

"Oh, no," Mona said instantly. "No way."

That would just spoil the fantasy, wouldn't it?

She hadn't come to Perfect Match to make an actual connection.

Ha! Virtual Bruce was probably nothing like the real Bruce. Heck, his name probably wasn't even Bruce.

No, it was better to let bygones be bygones. Mona had gotten lucky and had an incredible time, but really, how much did Bruce have to do with that?

Probably a lot, given how long you had to wait to get matched to someone before they partnered you with him.

Mona felt her resolve waver for a moment.

No, she was right.

It was better to leave anything she might feel toward this imaginary guy right in this imaginary room—well, no, the room wasn't imaginary, just the stuff that had happened in it was, other than the setup and the...

Whatever!

She knew what she thought, and what she thought was —*I had fun. Maybe I'll do it again someday. But I don't need to rely on a single individual I don't even really know to bring me happiness.*

"Thanks for everything," Mona said, slipping on her high-heeled shoes and standing up.

Argh, why had she worn those things again?

The instructions had been to dress comfortably, but she'd figured she would spend the three hours reclining, so it didn't really matter what kind of shoes she wore, and after spending a small fortune on them, she wanted to get her money's worth out of them.

Yeah, right.

The thought was that she was vain, and the damn shoes made her feel like a million bucks.

Vanity, thy name is Mona!

"You're so welcome," Leann said. "Would you like help getting out of here? I know the hallways can be a little tough to navigate the first few times. Many clients feel disoriented after their Experience."

"Thank you, but I'll be okay," Mona said brightly. "I've got it."

She totally did...

After four wrong turns and one attempt at entering a linen closet, Mona finally found her car, started it up, and drove back to her apartment through evening traffic that was quite bearable.

It wasn't until she got home that she bothered to

check her inbox, where she saw two emails from Perfect Match.

One was a survey, which, fair enough, they deserved, and she would complete it later.

The other...

It was a personal email forwarded through their system from Bruce Delacourt.

Bruce...

Oh crap, his name was actually Bruce!

The email was short and to the point but with an edge of sweetness.

Hey. This is Bruce, and I want to thank you for designing a truly incredible experience for us to share tonight. Your world swept me up the way only really great music has before today. I can honestly say that it was one of the most interesting and enjoyable things to ever happen to me.

I'd like to meet you and talk about it, and maybe find out if you'd like to do another Experience with me in the future. Only if you're comfortable, though—there's no pressure. Use the email address attached to this message to reply.

And thanks again.

Best,

Bruce Delacourt

Oh, dang. That was so nice. Mona sat down on her couch and stared at her phone, for once fresh out of ideas.

She didn't know whether she should give in to the tingle building in her gut and go for it, just email back and hope for the best, or if she should let her more levelheaded side stay in control and not bother.

After all, she knew nothing about this guy other than his name...and the fact that he apparently really liked music.

And he liked her story. That was pretty cool too.

Mona sighed and flipped over to her contacts list. She needed advice, and not from her mom, who would probably set her up with a rodeo clown if it meant getting her on a date.

Instead, she called her college roommate, her eternal bestie, and waited impatiently for her to pick up the phone.

Donna lived in California, for heaven's sake, she had to be awake—

Oh, hey, Donna.

The helpful witch in the story had been Donata. Wow, Mona's brain had been making all sorts of interesting connections there.

"Hello?"

"Help!" Mona blurted.

Donna chuckled. "I'm happy to, but what exactly do you want my help with? Is it your kitchen sink again? Because I'm telling you, girl, get a plumber. I am not the right person to call for anything involving a wrench."

"No, it's nothing like that. It's more..." How did Mona explain what had happened to her? "I met someone. Kind of. We had an Experience together."

"What do you mean by 'experience'?"

Mona did her best to explain the concept behind Perfect Match and ended up talking to Donna for over an hour about the world she'd been in, the fantastic details, the magic, the joy of being a dragon, and the pure romance of feeling so in love. "And that's the thing," she finished with a sigh. "Now, he wants to meet me in the real world, but what if he's expecting something I'm not prepared to give him? What if he's super gross instead of nice like he picks his nose at the table or double dips his chicken wings in the communal sauce bowl? What if he—"

"Mona. Babe. Slow down." As usual, Donna's calm tones worked their magic on her psyche.

Mona relaxed on the couch and listened to her best friend talk it through with her. "Odds are he's just keeping things simple. Surely, he doesn't want you to think he's some kind of creep, right? And you wouldn't match to a creep with this program anyway, I'm thinking. Right?"

"Right…"

"So, take it at face value—he wants to talk to you a little about an incredible thing you did together, and that's all it's got to be. You always get to say 'no,' hon. You don't have to talk to him, but if you decide to, you don't have to say yes to another talk with him, or dinner, or any of the things you're worried about. You don't have to tell him where you live or even give him your real name if you're worried."

She was right. Mona relaxed a bit more.

"And if he's the real deal, and you decide you want to do another Experience together, then that's great, and you can do that! Really, there's not a big downside to talking to him unless you're absolutely convinced it's going to end in tragedy for whatever reason, and that's fine too."

"You're right."

"Damn straight I am," Donna laughed, "just ask my man. He'll tell you."

"Lamar is a lucky guy." Mona had admired their relationship ever since it had started.

Donna and Lamar seemed made for each other, but she also knew how hard they worked to keep their love healthy.

No relationship was easy, and people needed to put in the work to reap the rewards.

"Bruce might be a nice guy. Just—hon, get your head out of the clouds of *'if if if'* this time and give him a meet. Or are you seriously worried that he's not as handsome as the dream king you imagined in your head?"

King Bruce was incredibly handsome, even more so than she'd imagined, and she had no illusions about real Bruce being even half as attractive.

"I'm not that shallow!" Mona exclaimed with a laugh. "Or… I'm not always that shallow!"

"Prove it."

"I will!"

She ended the call and went back to her email. Was she really worried about Bruce not being as attractive as she'd pictured?

Maybe, a little bit...but he had a lot of other things going for him too. At least, he had in her mind.

Ugh, she was never going to know one way or the other unless she sucked it up and wrote him back.

"Fine."

Hi Bruce,

This is Mona—same woman, different name. I'm so happy you liked the story we lived out together! I had a great time too.

I'm up for a talk.

She added not-quite-her-address because safety first, then finished the email with a simple sign-off. There. Now the ball was in his court.

Mona started making dinner, but her mind was on Bruce. He probably lived somewhere far away. There weren't a lot of Perfect Match offices yet, so people probably flew in all the time. He'd probably write back and say he wanted to chat over the phone instead. Maybe do a Zoom call. God, she hated Zoom calls. If she never had to sit through another Zoom call, she would be—

When her message alert went off, Mona practically threw her dinner parfait—what, it was a thing!—onto the counter as she grabbed for her phone.

Perfect. I'm just a half-hour away. Have you been to Vincent's Coffee House? They're really good.

Had she been? She was only there buying a cinnamon dolce latte the other day!

Sounds great. Mona dithered over the details for a moment before finally typing, *tomorrow? Around 5?*

Got it. I'll have a red ball cap on.

Oh, right. Of course, he wouldn't look exactly like he did in the Experience. Mona thought she would feel disappointed because Bruce had been seriously hot in there, but she was actually looking forward to meeting this guy too.

I'll be carrying a pink purse. Her vintage Kate Spade would do nicely. *See you tomorrow.*

I can't wait.

Honestly? Neither could Mona.

44

BRUCE

*B*ruce tapped his fingers against the tabletop, absently keeping the beat to the song he'd been listening to in the car on the way here while he kept his eyes open for a woman with a pink purse. He felt a little ridiculous wearing a ball cap indoors. Maybe he should have said a particular shirt or something...but this was his lucky cap. And if luck had ever been called for, it was right now.

Not that he was really expecting anything.

The most Bruce was allowing himself to hope for was to meet a person who was open to doing another Experience with him. He hadn't lied when he'd told her that what she'd designed had been the sort of thing he'd love to do again. If it was a video game, he'd have played it over and over.

As it was, he almost wondered if they couldn't go back there, pick up where they had left off and make it so that they were ruling together as dragons, with a kid or two in the picture to keep things interesting...

Now there was a thought.

Would their children have been born as humans or dragons?

Would it all depend on what form Charlotte—no, Mona—was in when she went into labor?

Would she have to change shapes mid-labor, or... shit, it was probably a dumb question because who wanted to put someone through labor when they were trying to have an Experience?

Unless maybe someone wanted to get a feel for it before they had their own kid...

A woman sat down across from him. "You look lost in thought."

Bruce looked up, saw the pink purse being placed on the table, and smiled at Mona.

She grinned back, and...yeah, he could see it, the way she resembled Charlotte.

She had different hair and a slightly different shape to her face, but when she beamed like this, they could have been twins.

"I'm just having weird thoughts about dragons and pregnancy."

God, what a stupid thing to say. Why did you—

"Oh my God, me too!" Mona exclaimed. "I'm so glad I'm not the only one! I spent most of the morning wondering about gestation periods and whether you'd have to nurse a baby dragon or give them soft meats to gnaw on, or whether they'd need to grow in their little teeth or be born with them!"

"That's a good question," Bruce said. "And would they want the meat raw or cooked?"

"I don't know. What did you eat as a dragon?"

"I don't think I ever did," Bruce replied. "But I remember dealing with some hunger pangs when I flew over a flock of sheep now and then, so I'd probably have been happy with raw."

"*Ew.*"

"*Ew,*" Bruce agreed. "Can I get you a drink? I don't know if you like cinnamon, but they do this amazing cinnamon dolce latte that—" Mona started laughing, and a second later, Bruce began laughing with her even though he didn't know exactly why. Her joy was simply infectious. "What is it?" he asked once he'd caught his breath.

"The last time I came here, that's exactly what I had," Mona said. "And yeah, it was totally delicious. I'd love one."

"I'll go grab it." Luckily at this time of the evening there was no line, so he was back in just a few minutes with two drinks and a piece of coffee cake to split.

Mona was staring at him as he sat down. "Do I have something on my face?" he asked a little self-consciously.

He wasn't nearly as handsome as King Bruce, and he was much hairier, but other than the beard, Mona couldn't see that because the body hair was covered.

"No, I...I was just thinking, it's amazing how much you look like the Bruce I met in the Experience. I thought you would be totally different, but you're... not." She smiled again. "That's a good thing, by the way. I had a wonderful time with you."

She was being kind.

He looked very little like his avatar, even though he hadn't requested that. He'd been fine with looking pretty much how he looked in real life. His ex might not have been satisfied with his looks, but Bruce knew he was attractive enough for ladies to give him covert once-overs.

"Same. Did you really write the whole thing?"

Mona shrugged gracefully and took a sip of her drink. "Not all of it. The curse part, yes, and the witch stuff, and some of the tragic background which, sorry about killing off your entire family, that was cruel of me in retrospect, but—"

"I didn't mind," Bruce said. "Honestly, it...I don't have a lot of family. Mostly found family at this point, so it wasn't like I felt that their absence was a huge loss."

"Ah. Same with me. It's just me and my mom." Mona rolled her eyes in fond exasperation. "She's the one who got me the gift certificate to Perfect Match. She thought I needed to meet people, and this might be the way to do it. I work for an advertising agency downtown, so a lot of my time is focused on my job."

"I totally understand. A friend of mine got me the

Experience for basically the same reason." Bruce was compelled to tell her more. "And because I think he felt bad for me after everything that happened with my ex. She left a few months ago, and I've been a little mopey since."

"Aw." Mona looked sympathetic. "Do you miss her?"

"No," Bruce said honestly. "We weren't good for each other, not really. I just missed having someone around. She and I didn't have that much in common, and I honestly think that I'm better off with her out of my life. She probably feels the same."

"Well." Mona raised her coffee cup. "Here's to breakups that are good for everyone involved." They clinked ceramic mugs and drank. "So...um. What do you look for in a person you're interested in partnering with?"

Oh. She was...wow, maybe she was interested?

No, she was probably referring to partnering in Perfect Match.

But maybe she was just as interested in him as he was in her?

Bruce smiled shyly and rubbed the back of his neck. "Oh, you know. Someone fun, someone who loves to laugh and makes me laugh too. Someone creative because it's always nice to have somebody to bounce ideas off of. Somebody who's open to hanging out with new people and wants to talk to me about their day instead of just closing themselves off." He sighed. "Someone who likes me. Who wants to be my friend as well as my lover. That's what I'm interested in. What about you?"

Her eyes looked a little glazed. "Gosh, those are good answers. Um. I'm also interested in being creative, because otherwise people get tired of hearing me talk about my work. Someone who doesn't mind tangents and sometimes appreciates going down a conversational rabbit hole. Someone who doesn't feel forced into acting like a gentleman but wants to be nice to me anyway. I mean, not like in a sugar daddy way, but the occasional act of holding a door or pulling out a chair...." She smiled and gestured to their drinks. "Or getting me a delicious cup of coffee. That's really nice."

Was Mona real?

Feeling very daring, Bruce said, "If you're interested in delicious things, there's a bistro a few blocks from here that makes the most amazing Filipino food."

"Ooh, the place with the stew! The one with the eggplant and the seafood, and it's kind of sour and kind of savory and...sinigang! That's what it's called!"

Bruce was dumbfounded. "That's my favorite dish there," he said.

Mona beamed at him. "Mine too! Should we finish our drinks and get the coffee cake to go?"

"That...sounds great."

"Awesome!"

As Mona got up this time to go to the counter and ask the barista for a box, Bruce stared after her, unable to look away from the woman who was so much like the person he'd known in the Experience, and yet so different too.

She had different expectations, different goals...

And he couldn't wait to get to know each and every one of them.

45

MONA

*M*ona was almost afraid of how well this coffee-turned-dinner date was going.

Bruce was...well, he was fun. Not as grumpy as his kingly persona, but with an air of seriousness about him that had made her wonder at first whether she was going to have to deal with the kind of eye-rolling and snide remarks that she got so often at work.

But there was none of that. He listened to her over coffee, bantered with her over stew, and now that they were back at her place—her place!

On the first date?

Was she crazy?

But she didn't feel crazy, and they'd gotten to the part of the night where Bruce seemed ready to open up a little more about his dating history and why he wanted an Experience.

"My last girlfriend always wanted everything to be

about her," he said with a little shrug. "And it's fair to want that kind of attention, I understand. It's natural to want to be appreciated. But I think that should go both ways and it never really did with her." He laughed a little. "I wasn't even expecting a romantic Experience, to be honest. I thought I was going to get to, I don't know, run around as a werewolf for a while and have some primal scream therapy or something, not get turned into a dragon king and fly around a kingdom managing disasters while falling in love."

Mona's breath hitched. "And...did you? Fall in love, I mean?"

Bruce looked at her for a long moment before answering. "I did...in the Experience. Of course, I knew it would be different out here in the real world. I'd never ask you for anything you were uncomfortable with. But..." He smiled. "We did have fun, didn't we?"

"So much fun," Mona agreed.

"Enough that you'd consider doing another Experience with me?"

"I totally would! I also..." Now it was time for her to be bold, to be honest. "I would love to date you in the real world, but I would also understand if you don't want to ruin the great thing we've got going at Perfect Match because it was pretty darn great. I had an amazing time, and if you want to keep that rolling in the virtual world, I'm cool with that. Well, once I save up a little," she added.

To her delight, Bruce's smile had become a grin. "I would love to go on dates with you."

"That's awesome," Mona said, "Although, honestly, I haven't gotten past the first date with anyone since I was in college. I have a bad habit of putting a lot of expectations on people when I first meet them, and it usually doesn't work out. Lucky for you," she winked, "I think we've already met quite thoroughly. So…yeah. How about we get to know each other in the real world?"

"I would love to."

To Mona's mild—mild, that was all she would confess to—disappointment, Bruce left soon after. He kissed her goodbye though, which almost made her feel like she was flying again as she headed for her shower, then to bed.

The floaty feeling continued into the next day when Bruce texted her to tell her what a great time he'd had and to ask when she was free next. Mona wanted to say "lunch!" but she also didn't want to come on too strong, so they ended up making a date for that Wednesday, Bruce's choice.

He went with a jazz bar, classy but surprisingly low-key, where they could talk and eat and listen to music without the pressure of having to focus too hard on being at an "event."

Mona loved it, and when it was her turn to pick, she decided to go classic and drag Bruce to a museum.

If he could get through the MoMA, he might just be a keeper.

He didn't just get through it. Bruce was an active observer and had some interesting things to say about one of Mona's favorite paintings, *The Lovers* by René Magritte. They bounced ideas off each other all the way through dinner.

When the date ended this time, Mona wrapped her arms around his neck, kissed him, and asked, "Are you sure you're ready to go?"

Bruce slid his hands around her waist, bringing her in close to his body. "Are you sure you want me to stay?" he asked, that serious look back in his eyes. "It's only our third date, technically speaking."

"I am." Mona knew as she said it that her words were a hundred and ten percent true. "This might just be our third date, but I feel like the person I got to know in our Experience and the person standing with me right now is one and the same in all the ways that count. That means I've actually spent what feels like months getting to know you, and every time you walk away, it feels like you take a piece of my heart with you." Her cheeks got hot. "Is that too much? Am I making you uncomfortable?"

"No, no. Not even close." Bruce moved his hands up to cup her face. "I feel exactly the same way."

When he leaned in to kiss her this time, oh...

It felt different. This kiss felt familiar, intense and passionate, not the polite kiss of a man bidding someone goodnight but the ravenous kiss of a lover desperate to taste her once again. Mona felt like swooning, but she held it together, giving as good as she got.

"Stay tonight," she said once their lips finally parted.

"Are you sure?" Bruce asked once more. He sounded almost agonized over it. "Because it's been so hard to walk away from you, and if you let me stay tonight, it will be even harder next time."

"So don't walk away," Mona said, amazed at herself by rolling with it. "Stay with me. Love me. Be Bruce the king, Bruce the programmer, Bruce the musician. Be everybody you are, and I'll love you for it."

"I already love you," he said and drew her into another kiss.

And he didn't leave after that, either.

46

BRUCE

*B*eing together in the real world was even better than Bruce had imagined. It wasn't that things were perfect—first-time sex was always going to be a little awkward, Mona's bed was really too small for two people to comfortably sleep in, and her alarm was set to something that made his ears ache. But going to sleep holding her and waking up next to her was pure perfection.

Don't fuck this up. Please, don't fuck this up. Bruce's internal voice lacked its usual desperate tone as he listened to it while watching Mona stumble to the bathroom—she'd stumbled in the exact same way in their Experience.

The thing was, as long as he was true to himself and didn't go out of his way to be someone he wasn't, Bruce thought that fucking up might be harder now than it ever had been before. Mona knew him, she got him, she wanted to learn more about him, and he wanted all the same for her.

When he'd left that morning, it was with the promise to come back tonight. At work, Bruce's rumpled outfit got few second glances—programmers weren't the most fashionable of people on most days—but Peter managed to look right through him.

"Okay, buddy." Peter leaned back in his chair as Bruce walked into their shared office. "You refused to talk about your Experience with me other than to tell me it was good." He crossed his arms over his chest. "But you've got to at least tell me this. The person you've been crazy over this past week, that's your partner from Perfect Match, right?"

Bruce hadn't wanted to confess much, but things were working out pretty great between him and Mona, and he intended to introduce her to his friends soon, so the cat would be out of the bag anyway.

"Yeah," he admitted.

Peter stunned him by whooping and throwing up his arms. "Hell yeah!" he shouted. "I knew it, man! I knew it! I knew you'd connect with someone there! Whatever their algorithm is that matches people together, it's *gooood*."

"Calm down," Bruce admonished, but he was smiling too. "Yeah, we're dating now."

Together for what I hope is forever, and as soon as it's not creepy, I'm going to ask her to marry me, but you don't need to know that yet.

"Amazing. Fantastic. That's just awesome." Peter sat back down in his chair, grinning. "I'm happy for you, man. You deserve someone who treats you right."

"Thanks." It had been a long time since Bruce had felt good enough about himself to agree. Yeah, he really did deserve that.

And Mona was…

Mona was everything he'd been looking for, everything that had gotten lost in the weeds after so long with someone who didn't really respect him and never wanted to see his side of things. Bruce was well aware that this was the honeymoon phase of their relationship and that Mona had never had one that lasted for more than a few months.

Things might change, and she might change, but the Experience at Perfect Match had given him the confidence to trust that this thing between them was solid.

Mona deserved the world, and while Bruce couldn't give her that, he could at least give her the best version of himself that he could muster.

Although, maybe he could give her more of the world if he was a king again.

Quietly, so that he didn't interrupt Peter or anyone else, Bruce took out his phone and texted Mona. *What do you think about booking another session at Perfect Match? Same world, so we could see what dragon babies are like.*

He was a little worried he'd gotten too explicit, but she texted back a minute later.

That would be awesome! I seriously can't get the dragon babies out of my mind. We need to see them in person.

Bruce smiled. *It's a date.*

EPILOGUE

"*Rawr!*" Tiny bare feet ran across the grass in Mona's mother's backyard. Little hands, twisted into a claw shape, made scratching motions, and a sticky mouth—Davey was always sticky when he visited Grandma—roared as the toddler pretended to breathe fire. "I'mma dwagon!" he informed his grandmother, who looked positively thrilled.

"Oh my goodness," Kaitlyn said, pressing a hand to her chest. "A dragon has come to my backyard! What a delight!"

"No, Gwanma." Davey dropped his ferocious persona for a moment and shook his head. "I'mma mean dwagon and yew a knight, and I'mma fight you."

"You're going to fight me?" Kaitlyn affected a shocked expression. "Oh dear, must you? Can't we be

279

dragon friends instead? I would much rather be a dragon friend."

Davey looked conflicted. Mona got it. On the one hand—fearsome dragon baby, *rawr rawr*, having fun running around and making people scream in terror. On the other hand—Davey was pretty well attuned to other people's moods, and he always preferred to compromise rather than make someone else unhappy. He was a lot like Mona that way—or, at least, Mona before she'd left her old job for a better position at another advertising firm.

She was a team leader now and did a much better job of sticking up for herself and her people than she'd been able to before.

"Um…"

"Dragon friends get Rice Krispie treats," his grandmother cajoled.

And that was it. Davey beamed at her and held out his little hand. "Fwends!"

"Mom." Mona rolled her eyes. "He's not going to have an appetite for dinner if you feed him sweets."

"You'd be surprised by how much a little kid can pack away," her mother said, then relented. "Just half now, then? And half after dinner?"

Her mother and son gave her matching hopeful expressions, right down to the wide eyes and protruding lower lips.

Mona laughed. "Oh, fine. Go get a treat. Bring me

one, too," she added, shifting in the lawn chair with one hand on her protruding belly.

At eight months along, Mona was in that awkward phase of pregnancy where everything she wanted to do felt like too much work. Just getting up was a chore, much less getting out of the house or chasing after Davey. At times like this, she was grateful she had a mother who was so in love with her son and willing to rearrange her schedule to come and help care for him.

A cool hand touched the back of her neck, followed by a kiss on the top of her head. Mona laughed and tilted her head up to get a proper kiss, then gratefully took the cold glass-bottled juice that Bruce handed her. His other hand was full of takeout—from their favorite Filipino restaurant, which Mona had been craving a lot this pregnancy.

"Good timing. Mom is feeding Davey a treat as we speak," Mona said, opening her juice. She took a long drink, then started as the baby inside of her suddenly kicked. "Whoa! Little Miss must like...." She glanced at the label. "Guava tamarind twist? Mm, good taste."

"She's going to come out of there craving tamarind, just like you," Bruce said. Instead of going inside to get Davey, or plates for that matter, he set the food on the backyard table and sat across from Mona. "How are you?"

"Hot, tired, and I feel a little bit like a beached whale," she said. "Otherwise, I'm fine."

"Aw. Would my cute, totally not whale-like wife care for a foot rub?"

Just the thought of having his hands on her poor feet was blissful. "Yes, please!"

As Bruce settled her feet in his lap and dug his thumbs into her left sole, Mona closed her eyes and basked for a moment in the fact that she had a man willing to do this for her. One who never balked at the messier aspects of childrearing or house cleaning, one who told her to do just as much as she was comfortable with and leave the rest to him, one who looped his friends—their friends now—into making sure that Mona and Davey, and any additional children they might have, were supported now and in the future.

Mona had seen his schedule of meal prep volunteers, and neither of them was going to have to cook for a month.

The thought actually brought tears to her eyes.

"Uh-oh." Bruce gently set her foot down. "Too hard?"

"No, no. Just..." Mona flapped her hands at her face. "Hormones, you know how it is. I'm just really, really happy."

"Ah." Thankfully, Bruce took Mona at her word this time because this was the second go around.

When she'd been pregnant with Davey and gotten emotional for reasons beyond her control, it had taken some serious discussions to make Bruce realize he wasn't doing anything wrong and that sometimes tears just happened.

Mona sighed and closed her eyes, taking another sip of her juice as Bruce rubbed along her arch. Their relationship was a work in continual progress, one where they were constantly learning more about each other. Fortunately, almost all of it was good. The parts that sometimes came up along the way, like his tendency to accept blame when there wasn't any to go around or her impatience with imperfection, were pretty easy to talk through.

Mona laughed suddenly. "Remember the last time you did this?"

"When did I...oh!" Bruce's voice lightened. "During our anniversary Experience."

"Mmhmm. I was pregnant in that Experience, too, remember? And I tried to fly...." She laughed harder. "And you had to catch me midair because my body wanted to roll! I was so annoyed when I changed back, so you had a servant draw me a hot bath, got in with me, and rubbed my feet for an hour. God, that was so nice."

"I assume a hot bath isn't what you want this time around," Bruce teased.

"Ugh, no. A cold shower, maybe. Or an ice pack."

"The next time we go for an Experience, we should fly north until we hit the ice sheets," Bruce said. "I looked on the map last time, and apparently, they're only a few days' flight away. We could bring some supplies for when we're human; the rest of the time, we could explore a completely different part of that world."

"How fun!" It constantly amazed Mona just how detailed the world they'd built in their Experiences was becoming. She had no idea when she first wrote her little story that three years later, it would include a thriving kingdom, a growing dragon/human family, and a world that always had something new and wonderful to explore.

Part of her wished they could go and do their Experiences more often, but with a toddler and a baby on the way, she wanted most of her focus to go to the family she was raising here and now in the real world.

"It will be," Bruce said. He worked on her other foot for a while, then patted her ankles in an indication of "I'm done." "Let me go get some plates and silverware, and we can—"

"Daddy!"

All orderly planning flew out the window as Davey, who'd just come outside holding half a Rice Krispie treat in one little hand, caught sight of his father. He reacted like it had been months since they'd seen each other instead of less than an hour, and ran over to Bruce, letting the treat fall from his hand onto the ground.

"Whoops," Kaitlyn said, picking it up. "Honey, do you want me to—"

"It's fine, Mom." Mona was more in the mood for actual dinner now than a sugary treat. "Do you mind getting plates?"

Her mother nodded. "I'll be right back."

Mona watched as Bruce scooped Davey up into his arms and gave him a big hug, completely ignoring the stickiness factor. "There's my favorite boy! Were you good for Mom and Grandma while I was gone?"

Davey began to nod, then he remembered his other persona. "No! I was a mean dwagon! Rawr!" He made biting motions at Bruce, never actually making contact—they'd had the "we don't bite people!" conversation enough times that he knew better now.

"A mean dragon? Oh no! What will I do?"

"Run!" Davey said. Bruce obediently set his son down, then ran away at a slow enough pace that Davey might still be able to catch him. Davey charged after him with glee, and Mona felt her heart fill to the point of bursting.

"It's a wonderful thing, isn't it?" her mother said as she came back outside with plates and silverware. She set them down on the table, then sat down herself and watched with a bemused expression the scene in front of them. "Having a family like this."

"It is," Mona said.

"I hate to say 'I told you so,' but in this case—"

"Are you kidding me?" Mona rolled her eyes. "You say it almost every time you hang out with Bruce and Davey!"

"Well, aren't I entitled to be a little bit smug?" her mom shot back. "After all, you and Bruce would've never met if it wasn't for that gift certificate that I gave you. Perfect Match was just what you needed to meet the love of your life."

"It was...definitely life-changing," Mona admitted. "I knew from the moment I met him in real life that Bruce was just as good as the persona I did the Experience with, but I didn't realize just how far we would go until it was a year later, and I was married and pregnant with Davey."

"And now you've got a wonderful son, a handsome and supportive husband, a challenging and enjoyable career, and a beautiful baby on the way." Mona's mother sighed the sigh of a woman who had looked at life and, for once, found absolutely nothing to complain about. "It's not that I wanted to push you into marriage and motherhood. I just wanted you to give yourself more of a life than work, work, work. You did all the rest on your own."

"No," Mona said, watching as Davey finally caught up to Bruce and tackled him onto the grass. Bruce rolled onto his back and gave Davey a huge hug, then held him up in the air like a glider.

Davey shrieked with laughter, arms and legs akimbo as he tried to balance.

"We did it together. Him and me." Perfect Match had given Mona the chance to create the life she'd always dreamed of for herself.

Two lives, if you counted their time spent as dragons.

She was looking forward to going back, but here was a pretty amazing place to be as well.

Ready for the next Perfect Match?

My Werewolf Romeo

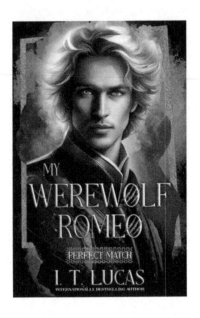

THE PERFECT MATCH SERIES

PERFECT MATCH: VAMPIRE'S CONSORT

When Gabriel's company is ready to start beta testing, he invites his old crush to inspect its medical safety protocol.

Curious about the revolutionary technology of the *Perfect Match Virtual Fantasy-Fulfillment studios*, Brenna agrees.

Neither expects to end up partnering for its first fully immersive test run.

PERFECT MATCH: KING'S CHOSEN

When Lisa's nutty friends get her a gift certificate to *Perfect Match Virtual Fantasy Studios*, she has no intentions of using it. But since the only way to get a refund is if no partner can be found for her, she makes sure to request a fantasy so girly and over the top that no sane guy will pick it up.

Except, someone does.

Warning: This fantasy contains a hot, domineering crown prince, sweet insta-love, steamy love scenes painted with light shades of gray, a wedding, and a HEA in both the virtual and real worlds.

Intended for mature audience.

PERFECT MATCH: CAPTAIN'S CONQUEST

Working as a Starbucks barista, Alicia fends off flirting all day long, but none of the guys are as charming and sexy as Gregg. His frequent visits are the highlight of her day, but since he's never asked her out, she assumes he's taken. Besides, between a day job and a budding music career, she has no time to start a new relationship.

That is until Gregg makes her an offer she can't refuse—a gift certificate to the virtual fantasy fulfillment service everyone is talking about. As a huge Star Trek fan, Alicia has a perfect match in mind—the captain of the Starship Enterprise.

THE THIEF WHO LOVED ME

When Marian splurges on a Perfect Match Virtual adventure as a world infamous jewel thief, she expects high-wire fun with a hot partner who she will never have to see again in real life.

A virtual encounter seems like the perfect answer to Marcus's string of dating disasters. No strings attached, no drama, and definitely no love. As a die-hard James Bond fan, he chooses as his avatar a dashing MI6 operative, and to complement his adventure, a dangerously seductive partner.

Neither expects to find their forever Perfect Match.

My Merman Prince

The beautiful architect working late on the twelfth floor of my building thinks that I'm just the maintenance guy. She's also under the impression that I'm not interested.

Nothing could be further from the truth.

I want her like I've never wanted a woman before, but I don't play where I work.

I don't need the complications.

When she tells me about living out her mermaid fantasy with a stranger in a Perfect Match virtual adventure, I decide to do everything possible to ensure that the stranger is me.

The Dragon King

To save his beloved kingdom from a devastating war, the Crown Prince of Trieste makes a deal with a witch that costs him half of his humanity and dooms him to an eternity of loneliness.

Now king, he's a fearsome cobalt-winged dragon by day and a short-tempered monarch by night. Not many are brave enough to serve in the palace of the brooding and volatile ruler, but Charlotte ignores the rumors and accepts a scribe position in court.

As the young scribe reawakens Bruce's frozen heart, all that stands in the way of their happiness is the witch's bargain. Outsmarting the evil hag will take cunning and courage, and Charlotte is just the right woman for the job.

Also by I. T. Lucas

PERFECT MATCH
VAMPIRE'S CONSORT
KING'S CHOSEN
CAPTAIN'S CONQUEST
THE THIEF WHO LOVED ME
My Merman Prince
THE DRAGON KING
MY WEREWOLF ROMEO

THE CHILDREN OF THE GODS ORIGINS
1: GODDESS'S CHOICE
2: GODDESS'S HOPE

THE CHILDREN OF THE GODS

DARK STRANGER
1: DARK STRANGER THE DREAM
2: DARK STRANGER REVEALED
3: DARK STRANGER IMMORTAL

DARK ENEMY
4: DARK ENEMY TAKEN
5: DARK ENEMY CAPTIVE
6: DARK ENEMY REDEEMED

KRI & MICHAEL'S STORY
6.5: MY DARK AMAZON

DARK WARRIOR

The Children of the Gods Series Sets

Books 1-3: Dark Stranger trilogy—Includes a bonus short story: **The Fates take a Vacation**
Books 4-6: Dark Enemy Trilogy —Includes a bonus short story—**The Fates' Post-Wedding Celebration**
Books 7-10: Dark Warrior Tetralogy
Books 11-13: Dark Guardian Trilogy
Books 14-16: Dark Angel Trilogy
Books 17-19: Dark Operative Trilogy
Books 20-22: Dark Survivor Trilogy
Books 23-25: Dark Widow Trilogy
Books 26-28: Dark Dream Trilogy
Books 29-31: Dark Prince Trilogy
Books 32-34: Dark Queen Trilogy
Books 35-37: Dark Spy Trilogy
Books 38-40: Dark Overlord Trilogy
Books 41-43: Dark Choices Trilogy
Books 44-46: Dark Secrets Trilogy
Books 47-49: Dark Haven Trilogy
Books 50-52: Dark Power Trilogy
Books 53-55: Dark Memories Trilogy
Books 56-58: Dark Hunter Trilogy
Books 59-61: Dark God Trilogy
Books 62-64: Dark Whispers Trilogy
Books 65-67: Dark Gambit Trilogy

FOR EXCLUSIVE PEEKS AT UPCOMING RELEASES & A FREE COMPANION BOOK

JOIN MY *VIP CLUB* AND GAIN ACCESS TO THE VIP PORTAL AT ITLUCAS.COM

INCLUDED IN YOUR FREE MEMBERSHIP:

YOUR VIP PORTAL

- READ PREVIEW CHAPTERS OF UPCOMING RELEASES.
- LISTEN TO GODDESS'S CHOICE NARRATION BY CHARLES LAWRENCE
- EXCLUSIVE CONTENT OFFERED ONLY TO MY VIPS.

FREE I.T. LUCAS COMPANION INCLUDES:

- GODDESS'S CHOICE PART 1
- PERFECT MATCH: VAMPIRE'S CONSORT (A STANDALONE NOVELLA)
- INTERVIEW Q & A
- CHARACTER CHARTS

IF YOU'RE ALREADY A SUBSCRIBER, YOU'LL RECEIVE A DOWNLOAD LINK FOR MY NEXT BOOK'S PREVIEW CHAP-

TERS IN THE NEW RELEASE ANNOUNCEMENT EMAIL. IF YOU ARE NOT GETTING MY EMAILS, YOUR PROVIDER IS SENDING THEM TO YOUR JUNK FOLDER, AND YOU ARE MISSING OUT ON **IMPORTANT UPDATES, SIDE CHARACTERS' PORTRAITS, ADDITIONAL CONTENT, AND OTHER GOODIES.** TO FIX THAT, ADD isabell@itlucas.com TO YOUR EMAIL CONTACTS OR YOUR EMAIL VIP LIST.

Published by Evening Star Press

EveningStarPress.com

ISBN-13: 978-1-957139-76-0

Printed in Great Britain
by Amazon